A Knight on his Bike and the Princess in the Tower

Ronald Blaber

Pen Press Publishers Ltd

Published in Great Britain by
Pen Press Publishers Ltd

25 Eastern Place
Brighton
BN2 1GJ

ISBN 978-1-906206-52-9

Cover Design Jacqueline Abromeit

Dedication

For the love of Priscilla Lewinna Jeanna.
The shadows grow longer,
but love's light remains constant.

About the Author

Ronald Frederick Charles Blaber was born in Sussex in 1920. At the age of fourteen he became an apprentice carpenter. A slump in trade eventually took him to sea, and he transferred to the Royal Navy during the war years. Returning to civilian life, he became a builder. Married with a family, he retired at 65 plus, becoming a writer of short stories and poetry for the fun of it. With failing eyesight, he is now registered blind.

Characters

The Petersons at 20 Mill Drive, Fern Bridge
Alex and Jenna – parents of Robert, Jamie, Ben

Robert's wife Sue, Donald, Lynn Susan
Jamie's wife Amy, daughter Verlisity Jessica
Ben's wife Mary – children Graham, Sally, Pete

Fern Manor
Sir Jacob Mathem and Lady Vivian – parents of Amy Linda

Amy's daughter Verlisity; her husband, Johnathan Percial
Old retainers – Albert, Mrs Page, Mrs Sumpling cook

The Fold
Mr and Mrs Hedridge – parents of James, Emma, Spencer, Gilly
Butler Stevens, Housekeeper Parkes, Cook Jannet
Uncle Sir Richard Gleasdon, James' wife Claire

Mr and Mrs Mason – parents of Andrew, and Becky
Andrew's wife, Rosemary Meadows Hall

Fern Bridge
Swales the Jewellers, Peaks the Greengrocer
Molly the Florist, Maggie the Dancing Teacher
Reverend Speers of All Saints
H. Johnson & Son, Paul – engineers
T. Hudson – farmer, daughter Mary

Glo-Tec Associates
Sir Richard, Jack Clevedon, Bob Miller, John Wilkes
Jim Fieldings, Peter Bradley, Lord Blenshaw,
Secretaries Jane and Mary
Housekeeper Mrs Roberts

Isle of Tess
Mrs Mary MacDonald, son Alister

In those few short years in which the old couple had taken up residence in the small seaside resort of Sol Cove, they had almost become part of the established scenery, but it was not as though they took part in any of the local functions, quite the opposite in fact. For they kept themselves pretty much to themselves; it was just the gentle, orderly way they went about their daily lives, there was a quiet dignity there, which made their presence both felt and noticed. Not in the least to those who, like the old couple, took their daily constitutional upon the eastern end of the promenade between 10 and 11 a.m. It was there, more often than not, they would be seen wearing those distinctive jackets of maroon and dusty yellow, arms entwined, leaning towards each other, with a flickering of a smile upon their lips, framing their quiet conversation, and for all the world like two old books – books, where every page was a tangled world of dreams, that only they could understand, but the music therein, was eternal.

Sol Cove was not in any way a fashionable resort, just a fair sized bite out of the Devonshire coastline, harbouring some 10,000 souls, this number increasing slightly during the fishing and holiday breaks. Its neat promenade, bordering a shoreline of rock pools and shingled enclaves, stretched between Sol Point and the breakwater, beyond which was the mouth of the river Fern and West Hill.

Almost two miles upstream, from the mouth of the river, lay a small inlet known as Sol Creek, complete with its Chandler's yard, jetties, and moorings for both the fishing boats and a few private yachts.

The town sported just one hotel, The Haven, and a number of guesthouses, plus the usual gift shops, but very little in the way of entertainment, its main attractions being deep sea fishing or walking across the untamed hills, and coastline. Other than that, it was an ideal place to unwind and relax.

A simple gravel track led up from the carriageway which ran around the base of Sol Point's grassy slopes, giving the folks who lived in any of the three bungalows which were built into the side of the hill, easy access to the promenade. It was here, in the large stone-built bungalow at the top end of the track, with its picture windows allowing fine views over the town and the surrounding hills, that the old couple had made their home.

Its neat and tidy gardens, both front and rear, were cared for by the husband of the young daily help, retaining all the designs and charm of yesteryears. The visitors, who filled the home with laughter, knew that there was no need for questions, the answers were there.

The town of Fern Bridge, and its market, was founded in the first instance to serve the farming industry, situated ideally in the central position of a long fertile valley and with easy access to the sea by sailing barge.

The pleasing appearance of its planned construction was achieved by the use of local stone, quarried from the neighbouring hills, and with the added charm of using reddish/brown clay roofing tiles, the whole effect gaining much favour with the local dignities who thereupon declared it to be normal practice in any other future development.

Overlooking the town, from the lower hills, were several large properties of which the most prominent amongst them was Fern Manor. The coming of the railway in the 1890s, (which terminated at Sol Cove) had brought a steady increase in the town's development which included both businesses and houses, all within its agreed boundaries. Whilst on the outer limits of the town, three private schools were built, namely St. Anne's College for girls, The Grange, and Benson's High for boys.

From its source the river Fern seeped out into a vast maze of tributaries before finally finding its true course, some fifty miles north of Fern Bridge. It varied its course and size a little during its journey, until it passed under the Fern Bridge from which it flowed through the western half of the town with its grain storage, warehouses and slipways for small craft, and from that point giving it a straight run to Sol Creek and the sea.

In 1947 most of the armed service personnel were home from the various war zones, only to find themselves in an equally difficult position – of how to handle this new-found venture, called peace.

In a pre-war, three-bedroom, semi-detached council house on the edge of the town, lived Alex Peterson and his wife Jenna. As one of those young veterans, it was not the peace that disturbed him so much, or his work for his former employer, H. Johnson & Son – as far as he was concerned that was the easy bit; he could now also cast from his mind, (with the love of his wife, and new born son, Ben) some of the misery he had witnessed.

To regain the fitness to his wounded body was what he needed most, to be there for Jenna, little Ben, and his two other lads, Robert and Jamie who born before he went away to war. This was what counted for him, at No.20 Mill Drive, to make that peace work for them.

With all the needs of a growing family, their future prospects never far from their minds, there was always a sense of gratitude to those nameless folks in the housing department who had put their names forward for the tenancy of No.20 Mill Drive.

They knew they had been fortunate with the house – the position was right, they had seen none better. It was a gem, the end house in a small cul-de-sac, with a stone boundary wall running along the side and rear of the house, beyond which was Hudson's farm and the great green belt of open countryside.

Throughout those uncertain years of the cold war, and the political pundits shadow-boxing on the world stage, while the

3

work force staggered from one political upheaval to the next, to their credit Alex and Jenna, like the rest of the good folks in this little cul-de-sac, kept their heads well down (they had seen it all before) and moved steadily on. The war had taught them much.

There was richness about their lives, a richness that others found hard to define. From that first evening at the local dance when he had taken her hand, his hair as dark as the sky at midnight, her tumbling auburn locks filling even the darkest day with the glow of a glorious sunset. They met, found eyes that were as one, dancing with the light and dissolving into a deep blue sea of endless time.

The past, to them, was always the other world; it was when they first met and were married, it was the world in which the richness of their love blessed them with Robert, a bonny blue-eyed lad with light brown hair, and two years later, with Jamie, with a cap of gold, a shade or two lighter than his mother's.

This new world came with the peace, its ragged war-torn edges stitched with the same rich thread that had woven their lives, to bless them once again – with little Ben, his golden cap flashed in the sun like a beacon, a child of this new age, a child who would make those lost years fade into memory.

They were a team, they were the Petersons; they fished in the north valley brooks, explored the surrounding countryside, and went on camping holidays. They gave the boys their love and understanding, be it games or school, and encouraged them into the love and importance of music.

Although the boys were protective towards each other they still, like most families, found time to argue out their opinions on whatever subject came to mind. There was never any malice in their arguments, more of a growing-up process, declaring themselves individuals in their own right. The one benefit the two eldest boys received during the war was being taught to read music and play their mother's piano, an exercise not only for the boys, but to keep her mind occupied in a bid to stem the worries over Alex. Being able to play the piano was an added bow, and they enjoyed the fact, and when Ben was old enough he also received lessons but was never that enthusiastic.

By the time Ben was established in the infants' school, he was feeling rather pleased with himself, sitting as he was next to Mary Hudson, the farmer's daughter, whose cows kept popping their heads over their rear garden wall. Ben loved cows. His brothers, Robert and Jamie, were doing well in the senior school and Robert, in particular, was already having thoughts as to where his future prospects were, while Jamie, always sitting curled up, with his head in a book, was on some distant planet.

But as it was, and I suppose should be, the field of play was already set out for Robert and Ben by their very location. Ben and his cows, the farm, the open countryside, the agricultural college, and of course, Mary Hudson, a bonny marriage, and family.

As for Robert, he always wanted to be an engineer, like his father. Alex was happy with that, the firm under Mr Johnson's son, Paul, was expanding, having acquired the adjoining warehouse for the fabrication side of his business, and needed young lads such as Robert, after he had completed Technical college, to handle the new metals and new methods of working.

Robert had chosen well, he had all the skills of his father and more. He was a clever lad, as the headmaster told Alex, "Your son is management material, Mr Peterson," but it did not stop there, and when a partnership was offered, he took it without blinking an eye. He married a local lass, bought a house on the edge of town, and raised a family of three; Donald, Lynn and Susan.

But what of Jamie, the boy with a cap of gold and eyes of the deepest blue, a serious, but talkative young lad with a winning smile that would melt the hardest steel – on which planet was he?

Jamie, like his brother and other young lads, had his paper round five mornings a week. He saved a little, but needing that little bit extra to purchase various books he wanted, he took on the job as a Saturday errand boy at the local greengrocer's and florist, which besides his wage included the odd apple or two.

He began to enjoy the job, almost as soon as he had started; it was so unlike the paper round – here you could meet the customers and have a chat, and of course now and again there was the odd tip. There were several houses and flats on the edge of town to which he delivered regular orders, mainly in the afternoon, and these were all in roads he knew as well as his own. What he liked best was the morning deliveries to the big houses up on the hill.

It was always a bit of a slog going up the first hill with a carrier full of vegetables, which in most cases meant getting off and pushing like mad, but there was all the joy of freewheeling back to town, with not a lot of traffic in that area. The world was his, he could be a knight on his charger, or whatever he put his mind to, he was in those moments of time a free spirit, leaping out of the pages of the books he loved to read. The last two deliveries he always made upon the hill were Fern Manor and the master's lodge at the Grange, both of them having trades entrances up tree-lined drives, cutting out the view of the main buildings.

The long drive at Fern Manor had a variety of trees and shrubs on the house side, and a tall thicket on the other side, terminating at the top with a huge bed of rhododendrons, which although the path went right around, the trades entrance was clearly marked to the left.

Sweeping up the drive, and around to the trades entrance for the first time, Jamie was met at the door by a very small women, about five foot nothing, whom he understood from Molly at the shop to be Mrs Sumpling the cook, and quite different from what he had expected; it was not her upright manner or voice that surprised him with that quick, "come

come come, boy," show of authority, but her general appearance. Her large ruddy face, with a frilly white cap perched on mousy hair which was trying to escape down each side of her head, sat squarely on top of an equally round body, giving her the appearance of a cottage loaf. To Jamie that day, and only to Jamie, Mrs Double Dumpling was born.

After his first few months in the job, he began to notice how quiet it was, up there upon the hill on a Saturday morning, and other than the cook (who still liked to hurry folks along, yet proved in fact to be a friendly soul) the area seemed to be almost void of people. It came as a pleasant surprise when cycling up to the master's lodge he saw two boys from The Grange, about the same age as himself, sitting alongside what he supposed was the school's bicycle shed, and being Jamie, called out a greeting, waved, and received a happy return.

The following Saturday, they were there again, sitting in the same place. So on his way back from his delivery at the lodge he stopped to pass the time of day, and tossed an apple towards them, with a cheerful apology for there being only one, "but," he said, "if you are here next week, I'll bring two."

Almost from that point onwards, the pattern of his life began to change, with or without his knowledge, such as his parents attending a meeting with his Headmaster, the consequence of which left them with plenty to ponder over, because before giving them any answers to whatever questions they might put to him, the Head was anxious to know what plans he had in mind for his future (the same as he had done for Robert), but there were none to speak of. At the moment, they explained, he had never given them any ideas on what he intended to do.

"I think you know from his school reports, what an intelligent son you have," said the Head, "but it's more than that of which I wish to speak about, it's his ability in the field of mathematics that is so outstanding, and is why in my opinion, he should go to Grammar School, and later to University."

Completely oblivious of all the questions and answers that were being banded about his future, Jamie with spring in his heart and the world around him in full bloom, swept up the Manor drive and around Roady Island (as he liked to call it) to deliver the day's order, with his ever present grin, into the waiting arms of Mrs DD.

For no reason at all, he turned left off of the drive, taking the narrow path around to the other side of the island which he knew would finally lead him back to the drive, and away.

This was all new territory to him, and he was surprised to find the area opened up a little, immediately after he passed the corner of the house, to reveal a white painted palling fence, and gate, surmounted by a pergola, entwined with honeysuckle and roses filling the morning air with their delicate perfume.

The same impulse which had taken him on this route, fuelled his inquisitive nature to investigate further than he would normally have done so. With the hand of fate now firmly on his shoulder, and the curiosity of a cat, Jamie propped the bike up against the corner of the house wall, lifted the catch on the gate, and stepped into the secluded garden. In the silence that prevailed within this corner garden, where the colours were crowded into shade by the overlooking house walls on two sides, and the large-headed roses with Cyclop eyes peering down upon him as though questioning his presence there, Jamie began to have second thoughts upon this day.

With his thoughts awry, but having come this far, he turned to the right and walked slowly down to the end of the path, and into the sunlight.

Week after week he had cycled up the trades drive, not knowing what lay beyond that closely packed hedgerow, and now it was all here before him – this beautiful colourful hedgerow enclosing the entire estate, beautiful green lawns with islands of trees and shrubs, and in the centre close to the main drive was a sunken garden with tiny box hedges, flowered borders, statues, and a gently cascading fountain, all of which he thought was truly wonderful. Then, taking one last look around, he quickly retraced his steps back to the gate.

Reaching the safety of the gate on a high, after his little adventure, he suddenly became aware that he was being watched, and with that he stood quite still, puzzled by his thoughts. He slowly began to rotate, casting his eyes in every direction, and it was not until he focused his gaze upwards, to a single light window directly opposite the gate, that his inner thoughts became a reality. For looking down at him was the bemused face of a young girl (at a guess, he thought, about the same age as himself), and as he looked towards her with a feeling of guilt, she raised one hand as though to acknowledge his thoughts, and it was at that calming moment when he was able to see her more clearly.

The low morning light that filtered through the windowpanes caught the sheen on her chestnut hair as it flowed in long tresses to dance about her head and shoulders, with every movement of her body.

The eyes that met and held his own in a steady yet gentle gaze, were of the softest brown he'd ever seen, bringing a smile to his lips; a smile which, when returned, transformed this unusual scene from one of vague suspicion to one of understanding, and a bond of friendship that had both method and purpose. Though at that time and age neither of them could ever imagine the journey or the outcome of this meeting.

Jamie's little escapade at the Manor, occupied most of his thoughts during the rest of Saturday, and into Sunday, in which there were so many questions, and answers; yet it was great to know what was on the other side of that hedgerow, and a chance to experience the garden, but through all his subdued excitement, there was still an element of guilt, especially as he had been caught out. There again, hadn't the girl eased the pain of that thought by the wave of her hand, and the smile? Even to a heart as young as Jamie's, the warmth of that smile had found a home.

His day was made complete, as always, by the usual visit to his friends James and Andrew, at the Grange bike shed, where he would sit with them as they ate their apples, and join in with their general conversation which also included school work. A lot of their various studies were all new to him, but as for Fern Manor – that was his own little secret.

During the following week, as the daily routine of paper round, school, and household duties, plus his leisure activities all holding prominence in his mind, most of what had occurred at Fern Manor was now history, but not the girl. His subconscious mind searched the faces amongst his classmates that surrounded him every day, and those on his journey home, just a passing world, a rose in the garden, and she was there, yet not.

Jamie was at the shop bright and early as usual, checking the bike before loading up because others used it during the weekdays. He was pleased to see everything was ready for him, and all the separate boxes which made it easy to deliver, and catching the smile on Molly's face he saw the order was larger than he had ever been given to take in one lot. But he was not too worried, for he could spend all morning up on the hill with his friends and enjoy the apples.

With a lot of huffing and puffing, Jamie finally made it to the top of the hill, and by the time he had completed the deliveries at the first three houses, he was shattered, and arrived at Fern Manor red-faced, and breathless, whereupon dear old Mrs Double D, provided him with a stool to sit on, and a cool glass of lemonade, which soon put a smile back on his face. Any further ideas of exploring the area had long gone by the time he had cooled down, so with a quick word of thanks, he made his way straight down the drive, and up to the bike shed, via the master's lodge, where his friends were waiting for him. They sat down to enjoy their apples, a casual friendship between two firm family friends and a lad they had taken a liking to, but who would not be a part of their future lifestyle. Yet from this meeting, and Jamie's gift with figures, that was all about to change.

For James and Andrew, this little hideaway at the end of the bike shed was perfect. Here they could sit in peace, surrounded by piles of classwork, helping each other to achieve an entry into Oxford University as both of their parents had in the past. In the half an hour he normally spent there, Jamie always managed to gain something from their work, and no one was more pleased than him when this morning's subject was to be ten questions on maths.

Picking up one of the copies from the bench, and with the approval of his friends, he neatly wrote down alongside of each question the working method for obtaining a solution to the problems, plus the final answer, all of which took him less than fifteen minutes; he then spent another twenty minutes going over his work, and proving the answers, by which time, Jamie was no longer an outsider – they were now a band of three.

Saturday mornings could never come around quick enough for Jamie, there was always a warm welcome when he arrived at the shop, with plenty of the usual banter, even from Mr Peaks the owner. They ran a good business, for having received the orders one or two days earlier, they were all ready to load onto his bike the moment he came through the door; he liked that, and there was never any demand for him to come back to the shop before noon.

He made Fern Manor in good time, and after a few cheery words with the cook, set off towards the drive, but just as he was about to sweep around to the right of Roady Island, the sound of piano music drew him like a bee to honey away to his left, and back to the white garden gate. He didn't have to think what it was, he loved it, and his mother played it from time to time – Chopin. Waltz in C Major. He walked into the garden and stood quite still until the music stopped, then he looked up at the window. He was not startled this time, somehow he expected her to be there with that same smile which had haunted him for days. Filled with the music, and her smile, he almost burst out laughing at the strangeness of it all.

By her actions, the way she stood there and motioned him to wait before vanishing from view, he knew this meeting was going to be a lot different from the last. He half expected her to appear in the garden, but after a few anxious moments she reappeared to pass a small white envelope through the partly opened window, then with a final wave she again departed.

He cycled down the drive full of excitement, with the letter burning a hole in his mind, but determined not to open it until he was safely on his own.

Having a girl for a friend was to be a new experience for Jamie; there were plenty of girls at his school, and in his class, but they tended to group together, As for his friends at The Grange, being an all boys school, the subject was never discussed.

Finding a quiet secluded spot, in the local park on the edge of town, Jamie sat down to read her letter. The first thing he noticed as he opened it out, was the neat easy writing, very similar to his mother's, with each letter nicely formed, and the next was the sense of humour built into her initial address:

Hello Mr Sunshine,

I missed you last week, you rode right on by – why was that? For the want of your real name, which I dearly would like to know, I can only for the time being call you my Mr Sunshine, I do hope you don't mind. As for myself, I'm Amy, Amy Mathem, and I would very much like to know more about you if I may – I know you like music, for I saw the way you were standing there. Do you play any musical instruments, or dance? Perhaps you could write to me, that would be just great. Must dash, have to go to ballet lessons, see you next week.

Amy

Jamie arrived back at the shop, flushed with the events which had taken place that morning, only to be confronted by Molly with a host of wisecracks that further confused his mind, and at the end of the day no one was more happy to go home than Jamie. He took his time composing a letter to Amy, doing it in his bedroom after he had finished his homework, and as he wrote down his name and address he began to have a feeling for this letter writing, thinking how nice it would be to receive one through the post. He wrote of his parents, and brothers, plus the old Labrador called Bob, and Smut the cat, he also confirmed the fact that he liked music, and played the piano, then with typical young lad's bravado, he said he could dance, but not disclosing it was only with his mother, and never serious.

By the time the weekend arrived he was ready, at least he had a plan as to how he would deliver his letter to her, so with it safely tucked away in his pocket he loaded up the bike ready for the off. As he did so, he saw Molly cast some of her flowers to one side, only because they had broken or had shorter stems than she required, and amongst them was a bright yellow carnation; just why he decided to pick it up, he would never know, but there it was sitting brightly in his carrier, and the more he looked at it, the more he could see it being a part of his plan, the rest he would be able to obtain just before he arrived.

All the week his mind had been full of a plan in which he could safely deliver his letter to Amy, and now as he turned up the Manor drive, the prospects of doing so filled him with nervous excitement; he could of course send it by post, but that did not fit into his adventurous spirit. He stopped halfway up the drive to step through a gap in the fence where the thicket hedge had been coppiced, and from a stack of cut branches selected the longest and thinnest he could find, before remounting the bike and cycling up and around Roady Island, to leave it close to the house wall.

After making the delivery to Mrs Double D, he quickly made his way to the garden gate, picking up the branch as he did so. He guessed she knew he was nearby, because of the music, for it was that which had drawn him there during his last visit. This time she had chosen Tchaikovsky's mini overture, from the Nutcracker. As quick as he could manage he propped the bike up against the fence, secured the letter and flower to the thin end of the branch with the help of an elastic band, before lifting the catch and stepping once more into the garden.

He first took stock of the garden, making sure he was alone before looking up at the window, and there she stood, waving her arms as though conducting the music, her face wreathed in smiles. That prompted him to throw all caution to the wind by raising the branch and walking across the garden where, after jumping onto the stone plinth at the base of the wall, he lifted it as high as he could and was triumphant to see the success of his plan as her hand reached out to retrieve the letter. With that done he went back to the gate for the reply, if any. When the answer came, the impact of her action put his mind in a twirl, as her written reply floated down. She waved and blew him a kiss and, as he had seen others do, he caught it to place in his breast pocket, then with a final wave she departed.

As he rode away to complete his morning's deliveries, and find time to chat with his friends before opening her letter, his heart was singing like a bird. This was the carefree Jamie who found most problems easy to handle, but little did he realise that between those friends he had made upon the hill, the path of his undecided future was now mapped out.

It was not just Amy's radiant smile, or the blown kiss, but the added combination of her neatly written letters with all those questions and answers that fuelled his mind to enter new fields of thought, and where in those letters (each one signed with a kiss) she was his spur and had pointed the way; his friends at The Grange, benefiting from his friendship, offered the key at a later stage to make it all possible.

That evening after tea, Jamie went up to the bedroom which he shared with Robert, and went over Amy's letter again before unlocking his desk and placing it into a little tin box. The letter had been full of excitement over what he himself had written, the music, and the piano playing, with a big plus on the dancing, "If only I could dance with you," she wrote, "maybe one day." He felt awkward about his fib, and knew he had to do something to rectify it. With that, he went down into the front room and played a little on the piano before putting a record onto the player and sitting down in one of the armchairs to enjoy the music of Tchaikovsky's 'Waltz of the Flowers'. The next thing he knew, from his faraway dreams, was his mother's puzzled face looking down upon him.

Wondering if there was a problem to be solved, she said, "Anything I can do, Jamie?"

Stumbling from his daydreams, he blurted out, "Can you teach me to dance, Mum? I would really like to dance to music such as that."

"I know I've danced around this room with you, but that was just for fun," she said, "but if you are so keen to learn, I will buy you a decent pair of shoes, and you can join Maggie's dancing class, over the draper's shop in the High Street, and you can pay for the lessons yourself. I know her well," she added, "I think it's two evenings a week."

Jamie started his dancing lessons the following week, and took to them like a duck to water, with Maggie checking his every movement, lifting his chin up, and encouraging him with every step. As he danced, his mind turned to Amy and the letter, "Maybe one day," she had written, and he knew then that he was dancing for her and he would get it right, he was determined not to make a fool of himself.

When Jamie arrived at the Manor garden the following Saturday, he found he had no need to use the branch, for Amy having warmed to the idea of receiving his letters through the window, had already suspended a little red bag on a cotton cord for him to make the exchange.

The weeks passed by so quickly with all the letters, the dancing, plus the extra exam papers he was given, and from them came a visit to the Headmaster's study. The Head was happy to inform Jamie that from next term there was a place for him at the County Grammar. There was an extra surprise for Jamie when he found out that all his three friends were also on the move – Amy had decided to follow her mother's profession as an actress, and was entering a college dedicated to art, and drama, whilst James Hedridge and Andrew Mason were both heading into the same well-established senior college, with the prospect of achieving a place at Oxford as their fathers had in the past.

Jamie slowly made his way down the drive and along towards the master's lodge, and the bike shed, with Amy's letter safely tucked into his jacket pocket, his mind torn with the fact that there were only two more Saturdays remaining before Amy and his chums at The Grange moved on.

During their recent meetings in which some of their future plans were discussed, they found time to exchange addresses, and vowed to keep in touch, so with all their class work finally completed, the conversation turned to family matters and various other topics, none of which really concerned Jamie, for James' father ran a successful accountancy business, whilst Andrew's relations were merchant bankers. Although he added his own views from time to time, to what had been discussed, he knew where he stood as regards to family, and was justly proud of his father, for he had skills that were in place long before money or pens and paper were invented.

Amy's letters were also of a similar approach – they were more searching as to his likes and dislikes and, in some obscure way, they were honing him into shape, which without knocking his lively nature made him take a closer look at himself. It was finally brought home to him when she wanted to know of his future plans in life, "What are your aims?" she asked, "where are you going, Jamie?"

He studied it carefully, it was the same question his parents had put to him on many occasions, and still wanted an answer to. It was one that found him equally divided in his thoughts, and ways, what with the technical ability of his father and the artistic values of his mother, so when Amy's question came before him he turned to the books he had been reading for a solution to the problem.

As he sat down to reply to her letter he knew, like the question on dancing, he had to come up with a answer of sorts. He sought an idea that would not only make Amy happy, but had possibilities for the future, and it came from a book amongst his father's collection – a study in engineering design and bridge building – which he had read several times with great interest. Without delay, he sat down and wrote to Amy of his intentions, and her response was electric, there was no going back now for Jamie, it was Amy's call.

Sitting down with James and Andrew, Jamie set before them his plans and ambitions for his future, his determination to enter university and to study for a degree in engineering which would lead him, amongst other types of construction work, to building bridges wherever they were needed.

One week on, and back to the bike shed where Jamie found his friends anxiously awaiting his arrival. From the look of their faces he knew they had plenty to talk abut, so sitting down quickly he produced the usual apples, and prepared himself for whatever they had in mind.

Speaking first, James made the point of keeping in touch very clear to Jamie. "It is most important," he said, "for if you make it to a university, and I feel sure you will, you might need the right contacts when you obtain your finals, and for that, either Andrew or myself could be your calling card to forward your aims."

It was Andrew who spoke next, the joker of the pack, "Do you dance, Jamie? I know you like music from our studies, but… dance?"

"Yes," replied Jamie, "I've been going to a dancing class."

"That's terrific!" exclaimed Andrew. "We've an end of term ball for the seniors at 7 p.m. tomorrow – would you like to attend?"

"That would be great," Jamie said, "but what about dress?"

"As long as you have a clean white shirt, black shoes and socks, plus a buttonhole – any colour – and be here by quarter to the hour, we will supply the rest."

Jamie made his way back to the shop, with a great deal of excitement coursing through his veins, and was barely able to conceal his thoughts for the rest of the day, a day made even more hectic with Molly's wild comments when he got her to fashion a buttonhole for him using a yellow carnation.

Alex and Jenna, perhaps looking back into their own lives, could not have been more pleased with Jamie's invitation to the school dance, although completely in the dark as to the boy's arrangement, so he left home wearing a white shirt and tie, black shoes and socks, grey trousers and a blazer, with his buttonhole carefully wrapped in his pocket.

He arrived at the bike shed just before a quarter to seven, and found James and Andrew already there, their excited faces showing eagerness to get started. Andrew fixed his bow tie, whilst James attached the buttonhole to his jacket, then they stood back to admire their work. "What a change!" remarked James, "but for the hair, even your own mother wouldn't recognise you. Let's go."

They went in through a side door which was curtained on the inside, in an area with subdued lighting, making it easier to slip in unnoticed, and mingle with the rest of the boys.

He had very little time to settle before the compère called for order, and requested the members to line up and welcome in the young ladies of St. Anne's college. At that Jamie's heart missed a beat – would she be there? he was asking himself. He felt as if he was in some sort of dream, as he stood there slowly clapping them in, searching for the chestnut hair, and the welcoming smile. And then he saw her – her gown of pale orange with half sleeves banded in gold, as was her neckline, with golden shoes upon her feet, and around her neck was a single strand of pearls. To Jamie, his Princess had come down from the tower.

He felt sure she hadn't noticed him, then why should she? For he was the last person she would have expected to be there. They started off with a quickstep, and as he was unable to draw her attention he took the first young lady in sight. This was followed by three more dances with various partners before they stopped for refreshments, but even then he was unable to approach her. He was beginning to get a little frustrated as they went into the second session, knowing he was being cut out by a big fellow who made for Amy with leaps and bounds as soon as the dance was announced. There seemed little he could do about it, so he went to the refreshments for a cool glass of lemonade, where his faraway thoughts were brought back to life by the voice of Andrew standing at his side, "What's up, Jamie? You're looking a little perplexed," he said, "can I help?"

As James joined them, Jamie explained his predicament over the question of Amy, and to their amazement, how he knew her, and how long they had become friends, corresponding by letter, and her proposal of a dance, with the written words, "Maybe one day". "Which seems never with the big fellow making his demands," Jamie said. "Not even sure if she has seen me with him around." Andrew looked towards James and nodded, then turning to Jamie he said, "The next dance after this is a waltz, and if you want that one with Amy, move up there opposite her, and we will do the rest – but move in fast, he's going to be annoyed, so it's now or never."

He stood where they suggested looking right at her, then raised the palm of his hand up to his shoulder, and it was only then that he knew she had become aware of his being, by the smile, and a discreet movement of her hand.

Standing there, happy in his heart that she had seen him, though slightly nervous of the situation in which he now found himself, with the big fellow a short distance to his right, Jamie balanced himself carefully on the balls of his feet, ready to make a move, recalling Andrew's words, "It's now or never, Jamie." So at, "will you," Jamie didn't wait for the rest of the compère's request before moving at an even pace across the floor, oblivious of the bustle taking place to his right, only conscious of Amy's widening smile and the anticipation of their meeting.

Slightly flushed, he stopped just in front of her, bowed, and offered her his hand; she took it with a smile, giving it a quick squeeze as he guided her onto the floor, still trying to convince himself that it was not just a dream.

Turning towards him she said, "Jamie, how come?"

He nodded to where James and Co were holding the big fellow at bay, and whispered, "Friends," and with that remark she put her hand up to cover her lips to stifle her laughter that was clearly there in her eyes.

As he drew her to him, taking those first steps, the faint scent of her perfume blended along with the music, enriching the melody, and dictating the importance of this dance.

So, with Maggie's words of encouragement firmly in his mind, he made every move count, in and out, round and around they danced, matching each other's steps to perfection, and as the perfume and music flowed through his veins like fine wine, Jamie was no longer there, he hadn't even been born, it was Alex and his beloved Jenna out there, dancing their way amongst the stars. This was no longer a dance, it was romance with music.

When the music finally died away and stopped, his spell was broken by Amy's voice, now almost a whisper, "Thank you, Jamie, thank you," and as he bent to look into those soft brown eyes to give his reply, he was called back to reality by the applause that was all around them, even the bandsmen were standing up. They were the only ones on the floor, they had been for most of the dance; as the dance went on, one couple after the other left to watch a little bit of magic.

Red-faced and overwhelmed at this reception they were given, he took her hand, and from where they stood in the centre, slowly turned to acknowledge the applause from all sides, then escorted her back into the company of her friends, giving her hand a gentle squeeze, and a quick word of thanks, before hurriedly moving back across the floor and into the shadows where he was gathered up by James and Andrew.

Both of the lads were laughing, more so Andrew who had tears in his eyes. "You've blown it, Jamie," said James, "I'm afraid you have got to go, everyone is asking questions, you were brilliant out there."

"It was just fantastic," chipped in Andrew, "especially the big fellow's face, he could not dance like that in a million years, he was livid." With that they led him behind the curtain, and out of the door. As he turned to go, Andrew's voice called out, "See you Saturday, Jamie – and the suit, keep it, it's yours."

Jamie raced around the building and across the yard to the bike shed, stopping only long enough to put on his cycle clips before grabbing his shoulder bag containing his clothes and riding away down to the short drive towards home, giving his farewell salute to the evening's entertainment by standing high on his pedals, punching the air, and shouting, "Yes Amy Yes!"

Arriving home, he put the bicycle away in the garden shed and went through the back door into the kitchen and, as he turned to lock the door, his mother appeared, anxious to know all about his evening with, "How did it go... Jamie?" then, "Where did that suit come from?" And, "Where are your other clothes?"

"They're in the bag, Mum," he replied, "and I have been given these."

Jenna ushered him into the back room, with a glass of milk, where he sat down and explained to them how he had become friends with Amy, James, and Andrew, and especially the dance. Leaving to go to bed, his mother followed him to the foot of the stairs, where he turned and kissed her saying, 'You're a good dancer, Mum."

As she lay deep in the folds of her bed, tired, yet fighting sleep, listening to the steady rhythmic breathing of Alex by her side, Jenna turned her thoughts to the events of the evening with all its implications – the surprise package of Jamie in that suit, a suit which effectively advanced his age by several years.

With it came the explanation of how he had obtained it, and of his friends at The Grange, plus of course Amy, and finally the dance.

True enough, Jenna could see that in the first place, Amy, the daughter of the folks in Fern Manor, was just a visible pen-pal, but that dance had changed things for Jamie, if not for the girl. Jenna sensed that, not with just his goodnight kiss, that was normal, but his spoken thoughts that were purely of Amy, and it was this fact that concerned her a little.

Jenna thought of Robert and his girlfriend Sue, nice lass, they'd been going steady for over a year now, always popping in for a quick chat, and a cuppa. As for Ben, he never went anywhere without Mary Hudson, more often than not in their wellies, clumping across the meadows.

But Jamie, who always had his head stuck in a book, even when he was asked to help with the drying up of the tea or dinner plates, he'd arrive with a teacloth in one hand and a book in the other, and for him to leap out of the pages for a girlfriend she had to be out of this world, and it was the world to which she was born that worried Jenna – she didn't want her son hurt by some form of rejection.

Jenna turned the situation over and over in her mind, then went back through the maze of thoughts to her own situation – how she had once set her heart on being a music teacher (something she still did in a small way), until she danced with a dark-haired stranger, fell in love, and had three wonderful boys. With that, a smile creased her lips, she turned on her side, snuggled up to Alex and fell asleep.

As for Jamie, the hours seemed like days, and the days weeks, and from where he stood, Fern Manor and The Grange were a million miles away.

This last week at school, like most other weeks before the end of term, seemed pointless to many, and none more so than Jamie in his present state of mind. He went through the motions of his paper round, and schooling, with very little spiritual uplift to his being there, except when the Head called him to his study to congratulate him on his further progress, and wishing him well. Jamie liked him, he was a good Head, always available to talk to when needed.

Then there was the letter he was writing to Amy, it was still not complete, he had to find something more to say or do, since it might be the last he could send in this way, and he didn't want to lose contact.

Walking the long way home from school, as he had so often done over these past few weeks, he was aimlessly peering into shop windows as though seeking an inspiration to his troubled mind over the coming separation, of not only his school, but his friends on the hill, especially Amy.

Their was no doubt it was these thoughts that drew him into the little bric-a-brac shop in the High Street, a shop he would not normally have set foot in; so there he was, weaving his way between the glass showcases, containing numerous oddities, and closely watched by a tall gangly middle-aged woman, with a series of stray plaits in her reddish hair, a neck full of glass beads, and with a multi-coloured dress of some Bohemian style, which left Jamie a little puzzled.

Jamie moved steadily up one side of the shop, and each time he stopped to look at any of the items on show, the woman appeared at his side, peering down at him from above the half-moon spectacles she wore anchored around her neck by a beaded chain. Her overbearing presence was beginning to unsettle Jamie, so he turned to make his way slowly towards the exit, and was on the point of making a quick departure when he noticed the tatty cardboard box on the shop counter, and a label stuck to its side which read, 'All items in this box 2/-shillings each'. Ignoring the hovering owner, Jamie decided to rummage.

The box contained a collection of cheap bead necklaces, coloured bangles, pill boxes, brooches, and various other small items, most of which Jamie knew came from house clearances and was added to daily. Although at first glance he couldn't see anything in there to interest him, he still decided to look it over, even if it was only to annoy this strange woman who, for some reason, had been hounding him all around the shop.

Jamie turned the oddments over several times, and was just about to call it a day when he lifted up the crumpled side flap of the box lid, which had been folded inwards, and from under it out popped a small brooch, no more than two inches long, covered with the hard dirt of years, and somehow he liked it, plus it was only 30 pence. As he picked it up to take a closer look, the woman who was still lurking in the background came towards him almost in a sprint, but pulled up sharply as the shop door opened and several would-be customers entered the shop. Half turning towards Jamie, with a sickly grin to take his money, but less happy when he asked for, and got, a receipt.

Arriving home, Jamie greeted his mother with the usual hug and a kiss, then after a few words on his day, went up to his room to change into his casual gear, at the same time placing the brooch and receipt into his writing box.

With the evening meal over, and things cleared away, Jamie made his way back to his room with the intention of adding a little more to Amy's letter but, on seeing the sad looking brooch, changed his mind by going into the bathroom where he partly filled the wash hand basin with warm soapy water. With the help of an old toothbrush, he began to carefully remove all the accumulated years of grime from the brooch and, as each layer was stripped off, Jamie became more and more excited as to what he now had before him. When he finally finished working on it, and wiped it dry, he took it back into the bedroom to check it over in a stronger light.

The markings he found on the back of the brooch more or less confirmed what he had been hoping for, it just had to be gold – but of what carat? That was something he could find out from Mr Swales, the jeweller in town.

The brilliant green long sculptured leaves on the face of the brooch danced with the light, their edges were also sealed with gold, lifting them into life, and at the top was a single headed flower, delicately crafted, and a shade lighter yellow than the main body; in its centre was a small white stone, and three slightly smaller stones were at the base, but for all its beauty the face that Jamie saw in there was that of Amy.

On the last day at school they finished just after lunch. Jamie raced home, dropped off his books, picked up the brooch, and headed for Mr Swales. He was a little old gentleman, who Jamie knew well from his paper round, and he had no doubt that the old chap would help him.

Making it to the shop was the easy bit for Jamie, but going into the shop and finding the right approach to the answers he required was another, even though the brooch, carefully wrapped in a clean handkerchief, seemed to be burning a hole in his pocket. Finally, after a few deep breaths, he made it through the shop door.

There were several customers in the shop, some being attended to by members of the staff, but no sign of Mr Swales, so Jamie moved over close to the counter hoping to draw someone's attention and, in doing so, finally be able to see the man himself. His luck was in when one of the staff came near enough for him to ask to speak to Mr Swales. Offering Jamie a seat, and asking his name, he said, "I'll give him your name."

Mr Swales appeared around the end of the shop counter, with his usual jaunty walk, holding his hand out to take Jamie's in a firm grip, and with a smile as always like a warm summer's day, "This is an honour, young man, twice in one day," he said, referring to Jamie's paper round, "what or how can I assist you?" he asked. With that, Jamie reached into his pocket and pulled out the brooch, then handed it to Mr Swales, saying, "I would like you to look at this brooch, Mr Swales, and tell me if it is of any value, or just a good fake." Taking out his small pocket magnifying glass, Mr Swales moved slowly over it, then turning to Jamie he said, "Would you like to follow me?" and walked back around the counter and into his office-cum-workroom where, after shutting the door, he motioned Jamie to sit on one of the stools by a long bench, while he occupied the other.

As Jamie sat there looking towards the old chap who kept making small sounds like "Ah," and "Ah," he began to wonder if the coming here was all worth the effort, and whether he might have been better off just giving it to Amy with the letter, for he felt sure she would appreciate it whatever it cost.

Still looking, Mr Swales cocked his head to face Jamie and said, "Yours?"

"Yes," Jamie replied, "I bought it."

With that the old chap spluttered, "You bought it?"

"Yes," Jamie replied, "from the bric-a-brac shop, and here is the receipt," he added, then handed over the small till slip to the jeweller. Looking at it, then looking back at Jamie, he burst out laughing then with tears in his eyes he said, "I'm sure Madam Butterfly would be tearing her wings off if she ever discovers what she has sold you for 2/-shillings," he chuckled, then continued, "I think you'd better sit there and explain the sale all to me, and then I will in turn give you all the good news, which I'm sure you're wanting to hear about your beautiful brooch."

Jamie sat there and talked over yesterday's walk around the town, looking for a small gift to give to a departing friend, and how he'd walked into the bric-a-brac shop and was hounded by the owner making him want to leave in a hurry, and also how he had picked up the dirty brooch from the box, one because it was only 2/-shillings, and for a second reason there was something about the shape he liked.

Still chuckling, and moving his head from side to side at Jamie's encounter with Madam Butterfly, he stood up and walked over to Jamie, warmly shaking his hand at his related experience.

The old chap went back to his stool, then turned towards Jamie, and said, "Now is the time to tell you all about your brooch, young man, at least as much as I'm able to. The main body of the brooch is 18 carat gold, whilst that clever flower is 12 carat white gold. The stones at the base, and in the centre of the flower, are real diamonds of good quality, and the leaves are formed from fine pieces of emerald set in platinum. In all, a very fine piece of jewellery, and at least eighty years old, not made for a shop counter, but designed and made as a special gift – maybe of love. As to its value, I'm not prepared to guess, but an awful lot more than 2/-shillings."

Jamie sat there in bodily form only, his mind and thoughts were elsewhere, then they had been since the dance, he just wanted a little something for Amy, but this brooch! What was he saying? "Jamie," then the voice came again with, "as you can see, from what I have told you about your brooch, the value of it is considerable, and you're a very lucky young man."

"Thank you, Sir," replied Jamie, hardly knowing how to express himself, or even come to terms upon what he had just been told, and then Mr Swales spoke again, "Would you like me to get the brooch valued?"

"No thank you, Sir," replied Jamie.

"Then what do you intend to do with it?" said Mr Swales."

"Well, Sir," said Jamie, "I came into town to buy a gift for my friend, and what I bought in a hurry cost 2/-shillings, and so I will stand by my original intentions, and give it to her with my farewell letter tomorrow."

The old chap looked stunned, "I can't stop you from doing that," he said, "No one can, it's your decision, but think carefully."

"I can understand your words of wisdom," said Jamie, "but this is something I have to do," and continued, "didn't I read somewhere that the value of any gift, is in the giving."

After a brief fact-finding conversation over Jamie's own future, without a doubt based on his concern for the brooch, the old chap finally asked Jamie if he would, in all confidence, trust him with the name of his young lady friend.

In that request, Jamie saw no harm in it, for as he pointed out to Mr Swales, his parents already knew about his friendship with Amy, and were happy to let it ride. With that information, Mr Swale's face brightened up, "Now knowing the family this little gem will be offered to," he said, "and of course if the young lady accepts it, then I will be less concerned, as to its future. But before you go, young man," said the old chap, "I'd like to add some security on that brooch, if that's OK with you?"

"That's fine," said Jamie, sitting down to watch as Mr Swales went about the process of photographing the brooch, marking the back with chemical dye, copying Jamie's receipt, writing a short note about the purchase of the brooch, plus Jamie's gift option, to which Jamie added his signature, and from there all the details were put into a sealed envelope and popped into his safe.

The last thing the old chap did was to put the brooch into a lined box, with the jeweller's name printed on it, and handed it to Jamie saying, "It is much better to give it in a box such as this, and with my name there; if there are any problems, they will come to me, and I will deal with them," he said. "Other than that, young man," he added, "I would very much like you to pop in and see me now and then with news of your progress."

Mr Swales bid Jamie farewell at the shop door, then stood watching until he was out of sight, before returning to his office addressing a staff member on the way.

"You know, Gerald, two little bits of magic in one afternoon, makes one very tired."

Jamie walked home at a fairly brisk pace, the feelings within him were similar to those on the night of the dance – he was totally elated. Tonight he could finish his letter to Amy, there was so much to say, and then there was the brooch, he had to put it to her that it was a token of their friendship, and if she could not accept as such, perhaps she would keep it until they danced again. *Wherever you are, please keep in touch, and I will reply, thank you for lighting my way. Jamie.*

It was a day full of light, and warm scented blossoms, a day to walk hand-in-hand across the meadows, and picnic in the shade, skip through the rock pools on some distant shore, or fish in the lake – not a day to bid farewell, but not forever, at least not as far as Jamie was concerned, as he polished up his shoes to look his best. Jenna smiled to herself as she watched him set off to carry out his Saturday round, noting the clean shirt, and sporting a tie. This young lad of hers, who was forever discussing bridges with his father, was now crossing the bridge of life, and into manhood, he was putting on the style, he was in love, or almost.

Jamie arrived at the greengrocer's like a breath of spring, whistling away quietly to himself, until pounced on by Molly, "What's going on, Jamie?" she asked, "you're dressed up like a dog's dinner – I bet you're chasing little Betty at the Fern, like as not," she added, and as comments abounded Jamie fled like a bat out of hell.

He paced himself so as not to get to the Manor too soon, but soon enough to have a few words with the cook, something he'd grown to like, and he knew she did too. Although he had two more Saturdays to do at the greengrocer's, this would be his last visit to the Manor, and also The Grange because they were closing down for holidays, so dear old Mrs Double D had plenty to talk about, and presented him with a bag of freshly baked cakes, and with a promise that there would always be a glass of lemonade there for him.

From there he quickly made his way around to the garden gate, securing the bike before stepping into the garden to the pleasing notes of Schumann's 'Merry Peasant', and looking up into the excited face of Amy, blowing kisses through the air, her smile as radiant as a summer's day. As the kisses came he caught them, one by one, folding each one carefully, before slipping them into his top pocket then, without further ado, he ran across the garden and placed his letter into her little red bag.

A full eight minutes he waited there, hardly daring to breathe, thinking of Mr Swales and what he had said, that Amy might not accept the brooch – he hoped that was not so. Then he had also asked her to keep it until they danced again, he would be happy with that, because that could be a long way ahead, and by which time anything could happen.

When Amy finally reappeared, unsmiling, with her right hand opened across her chest, and slowly nodding, his heart sank; then her head began to move equally slowly from side to side, and lighting up once more with a smile that said it all, and at the same time lowering her arm to reveal the brooch now attached to her white top. At the sight of it, Jamie leaped into the air, and had to restrain himself from shouting. With those anxious moments over, he ran across the garden once again and collected her letter before the final goodbyes.

Jamie walked around the last section of Roady Island, taking a final look at the gate, before mounting the bike and making his way towards the master's lodge, waving to James and Andrew on the way.

The door of the lodge was opened by a tall gentleman. Taking the box of fruit from Jamie he said, "I believe you are the friend of James and Andrew that was at the dance on Sunday?"

"Yes, Sir," Jamie replied.

"Well if I'd have known that they had invited you, you could have stayed. I'm very sorry about that, but here is a little memento of the occasion," and with that he handed Jamie two photographs, both of them showing Amy and himself dancing the waltz.

The words of thanks tumbled out of him so fast that he left the master laughing his head off. With the master's laughter ringing in his ears, Jamie made his way towards the bike shed, wondering just what his friends would have to talk about, for at that point the morning had been a strange mixture of endings, and beginnings, and he needed time to think, and look back.

James and Andrew were as eager as always to discuss as many subjects that had come to mind, particularly the dance, and Andrew was still revelling as to the whole affair, especially the big fellow, but left the finer details to James, including the fact that it was the sports master who had taken the photographs.

In the first instance, Jamie was surprised to learn that Amy sat out the remaining three dances, and no one could persuade her to take to the floor. "She would have done so for you, Jamie, but no one else," he said, "and another thing, Jamie," he added, "she thanked us both for being your friend, and bringing you to the dance, so you are OK on that score."

"I can add little to that," said Andrew, as he bit deep into his apple, "except don't forget to keep up with your intentions, so that we may meet again, and who knows? We might even form a new society called 'The Appleteers'."

By the time he had finished work at the shop, Jamie knew it was too late to see Mr Swales and let him know of the good news about the brooch, that was something that would have to wait until Monday morning. In the meantime there was still Amy's letter to read, and although he was anxious to know what she had written, his mind was set on leaving it until he was in the confines of his bedroom.

Before venturing up to his bedroom, Jamie sat down with his parents and, in the company of them and his two brothers, showed them the photographs of Amy and himself, upon which his spirits rose even higher, from his mother's face wreathed in smiles and the comments from his equally impressed father; "My what a grand couple you look," he said, then turning to Jenna he added, "I can read your mind, that could be you and me in there, my love."

"In a thousand dreams, master Alex," she replied.

"You look just great," said Robert, "maybe Sue and I should sign up with Maggie's class."

"I don't see why not," said his mother, "you might just be able to get Ben and Mary to go along as well."

"But without their wellies," chipped in Alex.

At last Jamie was able to sit quietly and read Amy's letter, a letter which by its thickness contained far more than normal, but like his own letter this was understandable, seeing what had occurred over the previous Sunday evening, and their coming departure, the thoughts of which had made him so methodical in clearing away all other distractions before he opened it.

He slit open the envelope and removed the letter, and with it came a short narrow box. He'd had plenty of surprises for one day, but what now lay before him in that little box left him momentary transfixed – it was a gold tie-pin, in the design of a treble-clef. He lifted it from the box as though it were glass. Jamie's mind was now working overtime, it was not only that the pin was gold, or of the musical inspiration that lay behind the gift, but the fact that she had valued his friendship so much when she bought it, as much as he had hers with the brooch. Now his coming visit to Mr Swales would have some added pleasure.

Amy's letter was in two separate parts, as he expected – the first part composed during the week, and the other after receiving the brooch, all in that neat tidy handwriting which he loved.

He read the first part of the letter, then re-read it again. Although they would not be communicating in the same way as they had done so far, she left him in no doubt that she needed him to correspond; she needed to know he was there, and how he was progressing. It was most important to her, she said, to know whether he was achieving all his aims that he'd written about, and if one day he'd build a bridge for her, to dance the night away.

What sort of bridge she had in mind Jamie was unsure, but the dance in itself, had meant quite a lot to her, hence the tie-pin to remind him of the occasion, and with thoughts of another day.

The second part of her letter was like an explosion of words to Jamie. The brooch, he knew from Mr Swales, had been designed for some young lady many years ago, was now being put under the spotlight by Amy who, somehow (probably from her mother) had a little knowledge of such items of jewellery, and made her acceptance accordingly.

My dear Jamie, Mr Sunshine,

Why you decided to enter into our garden, neither you nor I will ever know, but in doing so, you have become a part of my life. It seems strange, but the days when you never arrived, were sad days. You know a little of me, and I through your letters know quite a lot about you, and the way you held me, and conducted yourself at the dance, confirmed what I've made you to be, and that is why I will accept the brooch.

This is not just a brooch, Jamie, I know what it was designed for – it's a bond of love or trust, that although we may tread different paths through life we will always be there for each other if needs be, and because of my trust in you I will treasure it forever.
My Love, Mr Sunshine,
Amy

As Jamie read this last part of her letter for the second time, a band of steel gripped his chest, and flamed his thoughts. Besides his immediate family, Amy was now the most important person in his life, the girl he always thought of as the princess in the tower had given him her trust. He felt like shouting to the rooftops.

Jamie carefully folded the letter, and locked it away with all the others he had received, putting the tie-pin to one side to show his parents the following morning plus Mr Swales.

For Jamie, the next few weeks before starting at County Grammar became routine, and a little boring. There was still the paper round, and a bit of extra work at the greengrocer's, plus the occasional fishing trips, and when the day arrived to join the Grammar, he was singing like a bird.

After two years of good results at the Grammar, Jamie was offered a place at Cambridge University studying Engineering Science, and from there, with dogged determination to achieve his goals, he broadened his field wherever possible into Metallurgy, Geology, and draughtsmanship, though still finding time to join in student discussion groups and recreation facilities. But for real relaxation he'd seek out a piano, lift up the lid, turn to whoever was there and say, "May I?" and from their nod, sit down and play for at least an hour before closing the lid, and with a quiet "Thank you," walk back to the digs.

James and Andrew made it through to Oxford, as was expected, and even demanded of them for if either one or both of them were to have failed it would be deemed to be a disaster between their families. Their own personal friendship went far beyond that of the college, they were family friends; their homes were a few miles apart from each other on the Surrey-Sussex border, the families played golf and went out riding together, plus the family businesses worked in conjunction with one another.

Jamie, on the other hand, spent most of his mid-term breaks at home, and more often than not he could be found working with his father and brother either on the shop floor or in the office of H. Johnson & Son, to earn extra cash for books and other necessary essentials. Although Jamie and his friends were poles apart in the social bracket, they still held firm to the enjoyable fact of contacting each other whenever possible, either by mail, phone, or the occasional varsity events.

Likewise Amy's letters, which arrived at least once a month and occasionally the odd extra ones in between, were full of warmth and excitement of her everyday life at the Art and Drama College, going into so much detailed description of everything around her, that he almost felt he was there; and from his letters to her she highlighted points in his own progress, adding further words of encouragement as she had done since the very beginning of their friendship.

As with the university, Amy's college had both male and female students, which in her world of drama prepared her fully for the stage. After spending two years there they were offered small bit parts in various plays and musicals, each time gaining valuable experience before heading for the ruthless world of stage that can shatter dreams.

Although Amy had the advantage of having an actress mother, she drove herself ever forward, as she had done so to Jamie, and all her press reviews were full of praise. Amy was now on her way to be up there with the best. Jamie felt a sense of pride in her achievements, making the point of seeing her on stage at every opportunity.

During his last year at university, Jamie was invited by James' parents to spend a part of his mid-term break with them, which also included Andrew. They'd heard so much about him and were eager to find out more for themselves, the thought of which had already crossed his mind before he even stepped through the front entrance doors – any worries of what he was, or who he was, would now be purely theirs, for the years he had spent at the college had made him a very confident young man, and he now took these sort of situations with the ease of a diplomat. Knowing Jamie had accepted the invitation, James sent him a brief message as to what clothes he should bring, mainly concerning evening wear, for as he pointed out they kept staff, and dinner was

37

always a formal occasion, a tradition his mother fondly adhered to.

In many aspects 'The Fold' was as grand as Fern Manor, and the grounds, even without the formal gardens of the Manor, were equally as beautiful and very extensive with paddocks and wooded areas which in the autumn, Jamie surmised, would be a riot of colour.

On arrival, Jamie was greeted warmly by James' parents, Mr and Mrs Hedridge, who quickly introduced him to the other members of the family – Spencer, James' younger brother, and his two sisters, the eldest being Emma, next in line after James, and seven-year-old Gilly who, like his own brother Ben, was the most talkative one of the clan and at the mention of her name immediately stepped forward and took his hand. Looking up at him with eyes as blue as the summer's sky, she said, "Is it alright if I call you Uncle Jamie?"

"That's fine by me," Jamie replied.

"Great," she added, and strode away into the house.

To complete the formalities, he was introduced to the three most important persons in such an establishment as this – Stevens the Butler, Mrs Parkes the Housekeeper, and a fine looking woman called Jannet, the Cook.

With James and Andrew keeping him company, Jamie was enjoying ever minute of his stay at the house, and the dinner each evening proved to be something special as James said it would, particularly when taking coffee in the drawing-room after the meal. It was a large and very beautiful room, full of elegant furniture and fine oil paintings, but of all the items there, and through each evening's enjoyable conversation with James' parents, his mind was held by the sight of the grand piano that stood at the far end of the room – he wondered when, or if, it was ever played.

The answer to his thoughts came at the very end of the first of his two weeks' stay, for a dinner party had been arranged which was to include Andrew and his parents,

James' uncle Sir Richard Gleasdon and his wife, plus some business friends, and according to James, his sisters were going to play a little of the piano and violin.

After church service on that Sunday morning, Andrew and his sister Becky joined them back at the house for a light lunch, followed by a leisurely walk around the estate, making their way along the woodland paths to sit on fallen trees in a circle of light, and discuss the challenges that lay ahead for all five of them.

They arrived back at the house to enjoy a quick cup of tea, after which Andrew and Becky made their way home to prepare to come back for this evening's dinner. It had been a wonderful day so far, and a relaxed Jamie was loving every moment of it.

What he had learnt from this afternoon's conversation was a little more as to why he had been invited here – this was not entirely to do with meeting James' parents, but getting him close enough to talk to Sir Richard, and for that reason he was also placed next to him at the dinner table.

Jamie remembered well the last meeting he had with James and Andrew in the bike shed. They mentioned in that final part of their conversation of various contacts within their circle who could point the way to all he hoped to achieve, and Sir Richard was on top of the list.

When the big moment came, Sir Richard was not the tall elegant man he had expected, but a slightly balding gentleman of average height, making up for his looks by a sprightly step and a quick wit, putting Jamie at ease in just a couple of sentences, giving him the impression that if he had to work under anyone, it would be such a man as James' Uncle Richard.

This was certainly a man who held the key to Jamie's ambitions. He was a senior director of a worldwide company, specializing in the design and erection of oil refineries, power stations, tower structures, and bridges, from simple footbridges, to swing, cantilever, suspension, double-decker, and multi-purpose, each one a work of art to Jamie, and here he was sitting and talking to a man who could make these dreams possible.

After dinner they moved into the drawing room for coffee, and what was to be a little musical entertainment from Gilly and Emma, on both violin and piano. The first thing Jamie thought was, wouldn't his mother just love this.

The programme was arranged by the two girls to demonstrate what they had achieved from their music lessons. Emma had been practising for nearly two years he was told, and Gilly for just six months, and very keen.

Gilly performed first on a small violin, going through her practice routine, part of which was a lullaby. She took her bow, quickly followed by Emma, also with a violin upon which she played a part of Vivaldi's 'Summer' from the 'Four Seasons'.

Gilly stepped forward again and, with the help of a few cushions on the piano stool, played her party piece, the same as Jamie had done for his mother at an early age. Once again she was followed by Emma who sat down and proceeded to play Schubert's 'Moment'.

Throughout the programme Andrew was taking note of Jamie's interest into each piece of music which the girls had presented, none more so than with Emma now playing Schubert's 'Moment'; he was sitting in a forward position, his eyes fixed on the piano, and his fingers moving across his knees, keeping in perfect time with every note Emma played. Fascinated by it he quietly drew it to James' attention, who in turn passed it on to his mother – the smile of delight and nod of understanding from her said it all.

Oblivious of all those that were around him, his mind filled not only with the beauty of Schubert's composition, of which he knew and had played himself many times, or Emma's excellent presentation, but the near perfect musical sounds from this wonderful instrument that held him breathless. As the applause for her performance died away, he found Emma's mother looking down at him with a bemused smile at his startled expression at seeing her there, but finding his voice when she enquired if he would like to play something for them on the piano.

He stood up, and before he could offer much in the way of thanks, the small hand of Gilly's folded into his, her excitable voice adding to those around with, "Come along, Uncle Jamie, don't be shy," and led him across the room to the piano where, once he had her seated just to his left, he sat down and ran his fingers idly along the keys, then with a wink of one eye he said to her, "This is for you," and played his version of 'Kitten of the Keys', filling her wide blue eyes with laughter.

"And now," he said, as he turned towards Gilly once again, "I think we should play something for the grown-ups, don't you?"

"Yes," she answered nodding.

"This should do the trick," he added with a smile, knowing full well what he intended to play and had tried it out on a small upright. But this wonderful piano was made for such a classic, so he settled down and gave them Chopin's 'Ballade' with all the passion for the music and the piano his mother had instilled in him, leaving him drained and almost breathless as the last note chased the air.

He turned to find little Gilly at his side, "WOW, Uncle Jamie!" she exclaimed.

"WOW," he replied, feeling deeply satisfied in what he had achieved, then taking her hand he reached out for Emma's so that the three of them could take a bow to the applauses for their entertainment.

James' mother swept out onto the floor, planting a kiss on each cheek, and offering her thanks, before asking him if he would play for them again next Sunday, knowing that he would be leaving the following day.

"I'd be delighted," Jamie replied, "especially on that piano, it's a joy."

"Feel free to use it whenever you choose," she added, "In the meantime I think my uncle would like a word with you."

Jamie made his way over to where her uncle was sitting, and was politely offered a chair. "Well, young sir," he said, "there's more to you than meets the eye, and that's without question after that little performance, and I would at a later date like to know a little bit more if I may." Handing Jamie his business card he added, "When you have completed your finals at university, and are still interested in my level of engineering, as James suggested you might be, please do not hesitate in giving my office a call, so that I can arrange a meeting. It's been a pleasure talking to you," he concluded.

Thanks to his friendship with James and Andrew at the bike shed, giving him an interest in other subjects not covered by his local school, Jamie was able to gain five grades at his finals, three of them with honours, which opened a number of options for him, including taking up a post at the university itself. But after enjoying two weeks at home with his family, he contacted Sir Richard by phone, and made an appointment to meet him in his London office, resulting in him being given a six months trial, based in a company flat on the South Bank, close to the main office, and cared for by a Mrs Roberts, the housekeeper.

Both Amy and Jamie were now almost ready to venture out, and see what the world had to offer them. In many ways Amy was set for stardom, she had all the talent necessary – she could act, sing, dance, and above all was truly beautiful, and with an actress mother in the wings, plus being financially sound, she could wait for the right part to play, there was no need for her to sleep with some randy old director, it was her life out there and, like Jamie, there was an added determination to succeed.

Arriving at the main office entrance, Jamie was immediately ushered into a side office, and introduced to a Mr Jack Clevedon, who would be his mentor for the next six months; he was about forty years of age, with a ready smile and a firm handshake. All that combined with the soft Scottish burr in his welcoming words gave Jamie all the start he needed, here was a man with whom he knew he could work.

During those first six months working alongside Mr Clevedon, Jamie was given a detailed insight as to how Glo-Tec Associates operated, which was what he later assumed Sir Richard had intended. In a very short space of time he was able to see how vast their operations were, with offices in various parts of the world, dealing directly or indirectly through the United Nations to the various governments concerned, making some of their contracts a little tricky to negotiate, which at a later date in his employment with the company, he had the unpleasantness to endure.

As an exercise to evaluate his capabilities in this field of employment, Jamie was given a free hand to make observational written reports on all the various sites he visited with Mr Clevedon, both in the UK and on the Continent. This included checking existing plans for defects, and working practices on site, and putting through his own ideas in design, be it high-rise structures or bridges.

As each of these reports arrived at the office they were typed and forwarded on to Sir Richard's office to be scrutinised. By the end of five months' reports, and a further check on Jamie's grade passes at the university, he began to read into Jamie's way of thinking. His mind had a way of combining both his engineering and mathematical honours degrees, making him not only a first-class design engineer, but a superb troubleshooter, and with that knowledge before him, Sir Richard put a memo to the Board that, whatever their plans were, they could not afford to lose Jamie.

The two weeks before the end of his six months' trial period were up, life around the company offices was a whirlwind of activity for Jamie, from the various discussions he had with Sir Richard, to attending a meeting with the full company board, which he fully understood from Mr Clevedon was to make the final decision as to whether he had a post with the company, or was shown the door.

The questions that were put to him were on a great variety of subjects, including did he play golf, and what was his handicap? (not too sure, he guessed at sixteen for that), and did he go riding? At that question his thoughts turned to the two weeks he had spent in the company of James and Andrew. "In a fashion," he replied, bringing with it the first sign of a smile that he had seen so far, but when one gentleman almost at the end of the meeting asked him his choice of music, he must have wished at a later stage that he hadn't, for Jamie's answers to that question left him completely lost for words, with very little else to discuss. Jamie was excused, leaving him happy with all the answers he had given, and for now all he had to do was to sit back and await the outcome.

When Jamie arrived at the main office the following morning he was ushered into Sir Richard's office by his secretary, where he was greeted warmly, and offered a chair.

"As I expected, young sir," he began, "the company executives were most impressed with your papers, and on hearing the answers you gave to their questions, they would be quite happy to take you on board," he added.

"Thank you, Sir," Jamie replied. "That's great," he added.

"The usual five-year contracts have been drawn up for you to sign," Sir Richard said, "and I trust you will find them most agreeable," he added. "They include the first year's salary, which of course increases each year at the date of signing, and details of expected yearly bonuses, plus assistance in purchasing your own accommodation once you have become established." He further added, "I think it best for you now," he continued, "to pick up a draft copy from my secretary, take it home, discuss it with your family if you wish, and be back here the same time next week," he concluded.

As he made his way towards the exit door, Mr Clevedon appeared from his office. "Congratulations to you, young man," he said, offering Jamie his hand.

"Thanks, Mr Clevedon," Jamie said.

"There is just one point I'd like to make before you slip away," Jack Clevedon added, "if you come back through that entrance next week, fully intending to sign that contract, then my name's Jack."

It felt good to be home again, and as soon as he could he went out walking across the hills, stopping at the local inns for refreshment, and also a bit of fishing upstream. As for the contract he erased it from his mind, until halfway through the week, when he sat down with all the family present, leaving his father to read it carefully through to them, at the end of which, his eyes focussed on Jamie, and his breath came in a long low whistle.

"You've worked really hard for this, lad," said Alex, "and the strange thing is, you needn't take it," he added. "You could walk away, go back to university, or any number of options that are there for you," he continued, "and having read between the lines in this contract and knowing what have achieved to date" he further added, "you don't need them but clearly in this contract they sure need you." he concluded.

After lunch and the usual goodbyes, Alex for reasons of his own, walked with Jamie to the station; as an old hand at hiring and firing he needed to make a point or two. "Listen, lad," he said, "when you go into that office, don't be in a hurry to sign, ask a few questions – it's your life – and put over that point you made about getting involved with planning and design of contracts," he added, "and whatever you do, gain respect from the workforce – they count. Furthermore," he added, "when you find yourself in charge on a site, be the boss, no matter who it is that tries to muscle in."

"Anything else, Dad?" Jamie called with a smile as the train was pulling away.

"Yes," Alex called after him, "Marry that young lass you've been writing to."

Jamie tussled with that remark all the way to London, dreams, dreams, he thought, but anything like that was a long way off. First of all he had to make waves.

Jack Clevedon paced slowly up and down the main entrance lobby, waiting anxiously for the tall handsome flame-haired young man he had grown to admire, and when Jamie swept through the swing doors, with a smile as wide as a barn door, his heart flipped a beat as Jamie held out his hand and said, "Good morning, Jack."

"A very good morning to you, Jamie," he replied, "and if you can make it to my office for coffee, and a chat, I'd be delighted," he added.

Giving him a quick OK, Jamie headed for Sir Richard's outer office where he met Jane, Sir Richard's secretary, a fine looking woman at least ten years his senior, and was quickly ushered through an adjoining door to confront Sir Richard in person. After asking his questions, and going over the many points he had discussed with his father, and received satisfactory answers from Sir Richard, he signed the contract.

"Well done," Sir Richard said, shaking his hand. "If you hadn't asked me all those questions, I would have had some doubt about you," he added. "Welcome on board."

As he walked away from the office, his thoughts were to his father. "You got it right again, Dad," he said to himself, "you sure did."

Having placed his contract into the company files, Jane took Jamie along to see his office. When he arrived at the door he was surprised to see his name in gold already on it. "What would have happened if I hadn't signed?" he said.

"We'd smash it down," she laughed.

He went in, and found it was similar to Jack Clevedon's, with intercom and all the usual office fittings. With that he walked around the desk, opened up his briefcase, taking out a twin silver-frame photograph holder, and set it down in the centre of the desk, and said, "That's more like it."

Curious, Jane went around to look. "Your mother and father I take it?"

He nodded.

"I guess that's you in the other one," she added. "Who's the pretty young lady?" she asked.

"Inspiration," he replied.

"A most unusual name," she said, and as she walked to the door, she said, "I must warn the girls about that one," and laughed all the way through the door, and out into the lobby.

Jane had made it clear to him that this day would be his free day, a day in which he should go around to all the other offices and familiarise himself with the establishment, taking extra care when entering the typists' office, and from the smile she gave, he got the message.

He had coffee with Jack, who filled him in with all the day-to-day workings of the company, his desk in-tray would be full as from tomorrow morning, plus what was required from its contents. All travel arrangements and necessary hotel bookings were handled by one of the secretaries, leaving him free to attend to his own personal belongings.

After a light lunch in the basement canteen he went back to his office where he sat quietly and, with all the paper and envelopes available to him there, wrote a few letters, in fact four – to his parents, James, Andrew, and of course Miss Inspiration…

Jamie knew quite a lot about James and Andrew from those days in the bike shed. They had been lucky to have had parents who could give them a good education, they knew that, and expressed so to Jamie, but now for them it was pay-back time, that is if they wanted to inherit the country estates and businesses built up by their grandfathers; their work from now on, until they were deemed to be fully established, would be greater than those of ordinary employees.

Jamie's grandfather had been a riveter in the Clyde shipyards, and his son Alex was the youngest of four, a bright lad who attended night school and studied to become an engineer. He joined the Royal Engineers which took him south where he met and fell for Jenna – the light, and love of his heart. As for Jenna's grandfather he was a travelling musician, until he stopped and married a head gardener's daughter, and became organist to the local churches. Their son Fred, Jenna's father, grew up to be a saddle-maker, marrying the lead singer in the church choir – hence the built-in musical talent of Jenna, giving their sons talent, and creative ability.

Jamie knew he had a love for Amy, but what had she for him? And who was she?

Sir Jacob Mathem, Amy's father, was born into money from overseas trade, and grew up spending most of his time talking about it in gentlemen's clubs, until later in life it was found desirable to find a pretty young wife to grace his arm, which in his case was Amy's mother, Vivian, a beautiful young actress. After Amy was born he went back to his club; a bored Lady Vivian went back to her acting, leaving Amy more in the charge of her tutors, becoming as Jamie saw her the princess in the tower.

She also had dreams, and from there the lad with hair like a golden sunset became her Knight Errant. She watched him through binoculars as he freewheeled down the hill, his legs over the handlebars defying gravity. She coaxed him with music, he answered with a smile that melted her heart, and with a princely flower he wooed her. The dance was more, much more, she chided him to seek her, the brooch said it all for her, it was a bond of love, and as she grew older the bond grew deeper – but did he love her? She had to ask one day, she knew that…

He swept through the main entrance doors bright and early the following morning, gave Jack a quick greeting, and made his way into his own office where, just as Jack had predicted, the in-tray on his desk was full of document folders. Slipping off his coat, and placing it on the hanger provided, he opened up his briefcase, and set out his silver picture frame as he had done the previous day, and from that moment on it became something of a ritual for him wherever he was sent. Before he could take a seat to pick out the first of the folders, a quick rap on the door brought a bright young face into view.

"Good morning, Sir," she said, "I'm Mary your secretary for today, and if there is anything you require, Sir, just press the red button on your desk," she added.

"Thank you, Mary" "Oh before I go Sir" she said, "coffee will be along around about eleven if that's alright with you Sir" she added, "Thanks again" he said, and then took out the contents of the first folder, with that Jamie Peterson had arrived.

The coffee arrived being pushed in on a small trolley by a beaming Mary who said, "There you are Sir I hope its to your liking", "Thank you Mary" he replied, "and would you kindly take those five folders that I have completed, to wherever they have to go for checking," he said.

Although looking a little puzzled at his request, she took them, and the next thing he was aware of was a double rap from the door, and Jane arriving with the folders he had sent, which she then dropped into the out-tray.

"Something wrong?" he asked.

"A little," she replied. "What you have there," she said, pointing to the folders, "is a day's work, and please forgive me, Sir, for saying so, but you are a bit like a racehorse that's bolted from its stable, and I would ask you, Sir, please slow down a little, or we will have a riot on our hands from the typists – and I think you've seen them, Sir," she concluded with a knowing smile.

"I'm sorry about that, Jane," he said, "but I guess I just got carried away with my surroundings."

She left the office, but within ten minutes she was back again, to inform him that the day after tomorrow, Wednesday, he would be out in the field, as she put it with a grin. "You will be away from the UK for at least three weeks," she said, "there are various sites now under our control throughout the continent, from which we require a full progress report on, and Sir Richard suggested you for the job. All the necessary paperwork has been prepared, which you can look through tomorrow afternoon," she added. "Your day-to-day dress is more or less as you are wearing at present, but you will need to take a dress-suit, for the eventful working dinner. As for protective clothing, and travel arrangements, I believe Mr Clevedon has put you wise on that," she further added, "So I now leave you in peace," and left.

As Jamie resumed his task of opening the folders, and laying the contents across his desk, he knew in his mind that some of those sites he was about to report on in the next couple of days would have been through this system. Companies that in some cases, as he had seen from these folders, had taken on civil and constructional engineering contracts that were far in excess of their eventual capabilities, and were now running into trouble financially. There were others, through bad survey reports and lack of local knowledge, that were held up from geological faults, or underground streams, all of which Glo-Tec Associates with its expertise from its subsidiary companies could take on board. It was for Jamie with his ability to read quickly through the plans they had provided, to give them some answers to their problems and, in making detailed reports, direct them through the main office as to a possible final conclusion to their troubles.

The life's blood of a little Scottish riveter, a diligent professional father, plus the talented skills of his mother's line, flowed through his veins like good wine and excited him. Like his brother Robert, he had chosen well, this was his life, this was what he was born to, and he loved it.

Amy's mother, Vivian, took possession of a large two-bedroom flat in Bayswater London. It was within easy reach of the theatrical world which she adored, and where she could also bring members of that same world to discuss promotions.

Sir Jacob himself never stayed there, preferring to reside at his London club, though at most weekends he would motor down to Fern Manor, where they kept a skeleton staff, occasionally with some friends for golf or bridge.

Amy very often joined him there, work permitting, to escape the world of false 'darling', even though she was now having to play an ever increasing part in this world of make-believe. Here though she could read the scripts, and study her lines in peace.

It was also here where she kept all the letters that Jamie had written to her, all neatly dated, and locked into a safe keeping box, and unbeknown to her Jamie was doing exactly the same. It was an invisible bond that held them together.

From her bedroom she could see the distant wooded hills, that in the autumn sun turned into a golden sea of light, where she imagined walking there with Jamie, and resting in some quiet glade, to tell her of his love for her.

It was a confident young Jamie that arrived back from his first assignment abroad. He knew it had gone well, and had benefited from the experience; his French and German were more than passable, but his Spanish required some brushing up. Sir Richard, he knew, had given him a chance to prove himself, and he welcomed it by putting his heart and soul into the venture.

His first stop through the entrance doors was to Jack Clevedon's office, where he deposited a bottle of duty-free Scotch on his desk saying, "Only to be supped with coffee."

"You better be here then," Jack replied.

He then headed away into Sir Richard's outer office where he was greeted by a smiling Jane. "Welcome home," she said, as he placed a small bottle of perfume on her desk. "Bribery?" she added.

"No," he replied, "protection payment from that lot," he said jokingly, pointing to the typists' office.

"I don't believe you," she replied, before ushering him towards Sir Richard's office.

That successful journey abroad was the first real step on the ladder for Jamie, and he wasn't about to let it slip. He knew full well from his own background, and his father's words of wisdom, that opportunities such as he had before him now do not grow on trees and have to be nurtured.

Like a man on a mission, he searched for and absorbed knowledge from all possible sources. He didn't want to be just a troubleshooter, though that had become one of his most valuable assets to the company, but also to be in on the ground floor of any new planning applications that were to be prepared, even going out with the surveying team, especially on bridges.

It was his interest in the general designs being placed before the company that stamped him out as a man to be noticed, and listened to. He wanted all structures to have character, by blending light and shadows with design to create the sense of life. It was in these discussions that some wag decided to put the letters JP in red in his hard hat, which in many ways did him a service.

With two very good years of work behind him Jamie, or JP as he was called now from his hard hat, was now in the position to apply for a company grant towards his own accommodation as per his five-year contract. They had been busy years for him, always on the move, in or out of the country with little breaks here and there, and apart from some musical entertainment of a kind, it was Amy's letters that put the stress to rest – they were moving, caring, and sharing all the everyday moments of her life, so that he walked with her in every line she wrote; trees, flowers, lakes, or shore, he was there, and he loved it. She always began her letters now with *My Dearest Jamie*, and concluded with, *All My Love Amy*, just a few words, but to Jamie everything.

When Jamie offered the detailed plan of the property he was interested in purchasing to Sir Richard, he saw his eyebrows twitch a little, no doubt at the initial cost, which in its location was quite normal, but on his second visit to the plan, his facial expression changed into a broad smile.

"A-ha," he said, still running his eyes over it, it was certainly not the sort of property that he had expected Jamie to come up with in the first instance, then as he looked closer he could see the logic in it, and was quite happy to rubber stamp it with interest.

It was a top floor flat on the sunny side of a park-filled square in South Kensington, with a good sized lounge, two double bedrooms, one of which was en suite, fully fitted kitchen-diner, and a fine bathroom with a shower, but what caught Sir Richard's eye (and he knew that it was for that reason why Jamie was so keen on having the flat) was a short flight of stairs that led up from the inner hall into a studio in the roof space, making him the perfect study and office. It convinced Sir Richard that Jamie fully intended to remain with Glo-Tec for a very long time.

All the curtains, carpets and other floor coverings in general, came within the initial cost of the flat, and apart from the usual cleaning they were in an excellent condition, as were most of the decorations.

Other than turning the studio into an office-cum-workroom, complete with drawing table under the roof light, for the designs he intended to do, he lived pretty basically, until right up and into the signing of his new contract with the company, before the flat was fully furnished to his own taste and requirements. This included a baby grand piano, which was purchased partly from the generous bonuses he was given, plus a 'thank you' gift from local government officials abroad, and to him that prize was the only significant item of furniture in the flat.

The signing of a new contract was but a familiarity with Jane bringing it into his office, and over a cup of coffee pointing out the increased salary, and bonuses, upon which he said, "With increased responsibilities."

"It's the name of the game," she answered, with a wry smile, and left.

By the time Jamie had properly established himself in his flat, Lady Vivian, Amy's mother, had decided to take herself off, and divide her time between Fern Manor and travelling around the world with her theatrical group, gifting the London flat to Amy who, like Jamie, changed it completely to her own taste.

She was in contact with good agents, and was now becoming fairly well known in her own right, both on the stage, and as co-star in several short films, although what she enjoyed most, and was good at, was playwriting.

Both she and Jamie were living no more than a stone's throw from one another; in their everyday lives they appeared to be running or walking on parallel paths, driven ever onwards by the demands of the outside world, divided by some invisible fence, their hidden love held together by those precious letters, and seeking a way through to what should be. They were blind to where it would end, but if it were just Roady Island, they would nest there forever.

He followed her progress throughout the years, hoping to see her on stage at some point; when he did, he sent yellow carnations to the stage door, signed *JP, with all my love*. He was able to meet her twice, but always in the company of others. When she saw him, she greeted him warmly, hugging him, and kissing him on both cheeks. There was always a feeling, to him, that she would have liked to stay longer, but there was always that damned taxi waiting. Likewise she had looked for him, after seeing pictures of him with his hard hat, wearing the blue and gold company protective clothing, striding about with a clipboard in his hand, she admired him, but not so much when she saw other pictures of him, standing on a steel beam, talking to a steel erector halfway to heaven, she cried tears of anger.

Each year brought fresh challenges to both of them, from Amy's polishing up her acting skills, whilst pouring over endless scripts she'd been offered, carrying its own kind of stress and taking her off to the Manor on several occasions. Once she ventured into Fern Bridge, where she found herself peering into the shop window of Swales the jewellers, her mind in another time zone. As for Jamie, the pressure upon him at work rose and fell like the tide, making it necessary for him whenever possible to return to his flat, where after a good soak in the bath he would sit at the piano, dressed only in his bathrobe and slip-ons, and play his joyous piano under the watchful framed photo of Amy, for at least an hour, whereby all the stress and tensions of steel would have left him in peace.

He gained the respect of the workforce in his first five years, as to his father's advice, and produced a good formula in the way of organizing each and every site under his management, all of which he built on, giving good results in the completion of contracts, and increased bonuses all around.

It was this sort of dedication to the work involved, that at the age of thirty-one he was awarded the MBE for his work in the overseeing of government contracts, both at home and abroad. It was a wonderful day, with both his parents and two young nieces with him at the Palace, and finishing off the day with a dinner at the Waldorf Hotel, later joined there by James and Andrew, and their young wives. However, to Jamie the best part of the evening was dancing a slow waltz with his mother, to the tune of 'Always'.

Moving well into the third of his five year contracts, Jamie was becoming a very wealthy young gentleman, thanks not only to his further increase in salary, and bonuses, but also the help given to him from the company's own financial adviser.

In such a position he had become a very desirable catch to many a young lass, and there were plenty knocking at his door, for it was not all work for him – there were the odd dinner dances and cocktail parties where he was sorely targeted, but not caught. One 'date' lasted two evenings, and the second almost a week; it would have been quite easy to accept, but the words never came.

Just short of his thirty-fifth birthday, which he hoped to spend with his parents at home, he received a call from Jane that Sir Richard wanted to see him in his office. He knocked and went in to find him pouring over a map which was spread out across his desk.

"Good morning, Jamie," he said, "we have a little problem which I would like you to look at," pointing to the map. The map itself was a section of the west coast of Africa, and alongside which was a detailed plan of a civil engineering project, that was already under construction, building a single lane carriageway to open up the interior regions for trade, the whole project put forward by the United Nations overseas developing department, funded by the World Bank.

"This project is just over one third of its construction," said Sir Richard, "and runs unfortunately between two warring parties, one of which is demanding the road bends to the right, and to pass through his town before continuing on its journey, and that's out of the question," he added. "So the whole thing has come to a full stop," he said, "and as you know Bob Miller, I can only ask you if you would mind going out there to back him up, and perhaps get it moving."

Under Jane's instructions, he went back to his flat, and put together all the necessary items he would need for what he hoped would be a short stay. He then ran his fingers gently up and down the ivories on his piano, before closing the lid and sitting down at his desk to write a letter to Amy.

Slipping the letter into the envelope, he sealed it and began to write the address, Miss Linda Fern, her stage name; it always brought a little smile upon him, for inside it read *My Dearest Amy*. Looking at it, his mind went back over these last couple of years when he first saw her with a young man on her arm, smiling towards each other, and whatever the papers thought, the smile was false. He knew Amy, the same applied to the second beau, a year later. She never mentioned them in her letters, which were the same as usual, all loving, and caring as though the rest of the world didn't exist.

He awoke with his alarm at 11 p.m., giving himself time for a quick shower before the company car arrived to take him to the airport, for a night flight to Lagos where he would board another plane to his destination. He finally arrived at 6 a.m., when a car was waiting for him to take him on to the construction site, and the living quarters where, after dumping his holdall, he stepped out into the steam bath atmosphere and made his way towards a large Portakabin marked 'Office', where Bob Miller was waiting for him at the entrance door.

"Good morning, JP," he said, "welcome to Glo-Tec Hotel."

"What's the service like?" Jamie said.

"Rubbish," was the reply, "but the tea's OK, so get yourself in here, and we'll have a chat over a cuppa."

A short while after Bob had finally explained the situation to him, especially the number of trigger-happy boy soldiers lined up across the end of the road, and a chappie in charge who thinks he's a general, and no sign of the real boss, Jamie suggested they rode out and take a closer look.

Ignoring the General's directions, Jamie noticed that none of the soldier boys were out beyond the left-hand edge of the new road. "They wouldn't do that, that's rival territory," said Bob.

"Oh," said Jamie, "in that case I think we may be able to push things along a bit." Sitting in the truck's cab, he quickly sketched out his idea.

"It's certainly worth a try," Bob said, "but it's likely to start World War Three," he added, nonetheless they went back to the office to prepare for the following morning.

The work's team drove several wooden stakes in, following the line of the new road, and stranded it with razor wire, and with the aid of a dumpy level, they made the pretence of surveying the left-hand side, driving in marker pegs in a wide easy bend, before calling up the JCB. Questioning their actions, Jamie painfully informed the General that as he had stopped them from going ahead, they were going to the left. He went ballistic, and so they made it back to the office to wait for the fireworks.

From there they made a call to the British Consulate for immediate assistance, informing them of their situation, and the threat of a possible attack, which wasn't too far from the truth.

Two hours later, on an open-top Rolls, swept into the compound, stopping in front of the office. A large uniformed coloured gentleman got out, followed by three armed men, and strode into the office demanding to know who was responsible in moving the road to the left instead of to the right. Banging his stick on the desk he shouted, "This cannot be allowed, I want that person removed," he added.

With that Jamie drew himself up to his full height, put on his hard hat, and said, "I gave the order for the road to be diverted to the left, Sir, and that's where it's going, unless of course you change your mind, and allow it to be constructed to where it was originally planned."

In silence they stood looking at each other for almost a minute before Jamie added, "Now if you've nothing more to say, Sir, I must ask you to leave my office, I've work to do."

With an angry snort he left, leaving Bob to explode. "Bloody hell, JP, he was going to shoot us."

"I thought that," said Jamie, "but he didn't did he, and as far as your road is concerned, I think its checkmate to us – don't you agree?"

After three weeks out there with Bob, weeks in which with the departing of the boy soldiers, and the recruiting of additional local menfolk to move quickly through the troubled area, Jamie finally made his way home, arriving at his flat in the late afternoon to inform the office of his intentions of being with them the following morning.

Jack welcomed him into his office, and showed him a newspaper's brief account of his exploits.

"Oh dear," Jamie said, "that's not going to brighten the day is it?" and proceeded along to his own office where, after sorting out the mail, he wrote out his report on the assignment.

Although Sir Richard fully understood the situation they were facing, and approved of the plan they had devised to lift the blockade, he stated, "The confrontation with the coloured gentleman, should have been handled by a Diplomat or local government official. I don't want my staff getting their heads blown off. Now, young sir," he added, "go home, and I expect to see you in two weeks."

With his thirty-sixth birthday slipping by, Jamie found himself in the Middle East, overseeing the preparation work to an oil refinery that had been damaged by terrorists. His duty there would take no longer than three weeks, before the construction team moved in to complete the job, but with the work well under way, he had an unsettled feeling running through his mind. Something was nagging at him, he made contact with his parents, and they were fine, and the only possible option left was Amy.

The thought that she owed him a letter made it more of a certainty to him so, after checking with the site general foreman, he flew back to London, informing him that he would return by the day after next, Saturday.

He arrived late in the day, going straight to his flat for a wash and change of clothes, before taking a taxi around to the Bayswater flat hoping she was there. He knew she had been filming in Spain, but that was in her last letter, so paying off the taxi, he pushed the button to her flat on the outer door's intercom panel, catching his breath at the sound of her voice.

"Jamie, how lovely, do come up," she said. When he stepped out of the lift onto a small landing, the entrance to her flat was immediately thrown open by an excitable Amy, looking truly beautiful in golden slip-ons, the palest of blue jeans, and a pink chiffon blouse. She reached up to him and kissed him full on the lips, which in some way led him further along the line to believe that she was in trouble.

"Coffee?" she said helping him out of his jacket, "or something stronger?"

"Coffee's fine," he said walking into the kitchen with her to help with the tray.

"What brings you to my door?" she said, after pausing from talking ten to the dozen.

"You, Amy," he answered, "I know you've missed a letter to me, but it's more than that, much more, we're too close for me not to know."

The Amy he knew was now gone, there was a more solemn and angrier Amy before him now. "It's my problem not yours," she said, "and my mistake."

"Try me," he replied.

"I was stupid, stupid, bloody stupid," she added. "I'm pregnant," she said almost in a whisper.

"Pregnant," he repeated, "If you intend to carry that child," he added, "never ever call that child a mistake, especially in front of me, or the child – you'll blight its life forever," he said. "The father of the child – do you love him?" he further added.

"Love them," she said raising her voice, "of course I don't bloody well love them," she added.

"Them!" Jamie exploded, "I think it's fair that I should know a little more about this, don't you Amy?" he said.

And with that she explained, how after the completion of filming, there was always the usual champagne party. She'd had about three drinks, and decided to go to her hotel room, but slipped out later to pick up a card from the front desk, passing the door where the party was still in full swing, when two of the actors saw her and insisted she have a nightcap, which was spiked. "I remember them carrying me to my room," she said, "and I knew something was happening to me, and people laughing, and when I awoke late next morning, I was full of pain, and they had all departed leaving me shocked."

He picked up the coffee tray, and carried it into the kitchen; she was sitting hunched up in a corner of the settee.

"The child," he said.

"It's alone," she replied. "Like I was, you remember? Then you walked into the garden, why did you do that I wonder? Sent me a flower, filling me with dreams, and danced me to the stars, gave me a bond of love, why, why, Mr Troubleshooter. Then you try to kill yourself, by walking about halfway to heaven, telling someone how to put a nut on a bolt, and trying to get shot in some stinking jungle – don't you ever, ever think that someone cares about you?" She was rambling on through a veil of tears, he knew now, really knew now, that she loved him, as much as he loved her. He put his hand out to touch her, she snapped angrily, "Don't touch me, just go, just go, I'll sort my own problems out, go on, go."

"If that's what you want," he said, "I'm around until late Saturday," then picking up his jacket he opened the door.

"You come back here," she snapped again, "come back, and close the door, and don't you dare grin, Mr Ruddy Peterson."

Almost lost for something to say, he dropped his jacket onto a chair, and walked around to the back of the settee, where he leaned over to kiss the top of her head. "I love you," he said, then turning to the piano there, he sat down, lifted the keyboard lid, and with his fingers barely touching the ivories, he slowed the tempo down to a minimum, letting his mind drift to blend with hers, and those early years, chasing the shadows by playing, 'When You Were Sweet Sixteen'.

63

He sensed the movement behind him, her hands fell lightly upon his shoulders, as she buried her head onto his. She kissed his cheek, and as he turned his face towards her, she kissed him gently on the lips. "I'll take a shower," she said, he nodded.

He was still playing when she joined him on the long piano stool, dressed in her bath robe, her perfume capturing him. She pulled him to her kissing him again, then laid a bathrobe across his knees, "There's dry towels for you," he nodded once more, and she continued the piano playing.

He showered and walked back to the piano stool, barefoot, wrapped in the robe she had given him, and then sat down once more alongside of her. She closed the keyboard lid, and turned towards him reaching for his hand.

"What am I going to do, my love?" she said, quietly appealing for an answer.

"Marry me," he replied.

"We don't own ourselves you, and I," she said, "We belong to the world, they lay demands upon us, you know that, my love," she added.

He bowed his head to her reckoning, and said, "There has to be a way for us and the little one, there has to be."

She stood up, took his hand, and walked slowly across the floor, and into her bedroom, pulling back the sheets. She let the robe slip to the floor, removing his they stood motionless, then she embraced him, and the lips that found his, set the blood racing to his loins filling him with desire.

She took him to her bed, where they lay on their sides facing each other in silence, as she ran her fingers through his hair, with her eyes melting into his, she said, "I love you."

"I know," he replied, and then putting out the light, they moved into each other's arms.

He showered her face, and neck with soft gentle kisses, and bathed in the passion of her sensuous kisses upon his own. He caressed her to him as she responded to his touch. The sweet softness of her body led him on to greater heights of ecstasy; he caught the short intake of her breath, as he touched and kissed her breasts, letting his lips run across her nipples, so firm with emotional rapture, as her long caresses slipped down to his loins, and found his proud manhood. She pushed her leg over his body, and guided it into her, and held him tight, neither of them wanted to devour each other. They had waited far too long for this moment, and expressed their joy when the richness of all creation broke free and washed over them as the tide of time, casting the lust that was once theirs, leaving in its wake the true love for each other. They clung even tighter, for fear it might slip away beyond that invisible curtain of the years of wanting, until drained they found the peace of body, mind, and soul, and slept.

Woken by the soft warm breath that touched his brow, Jamie opened one eye to see the smiling face of Amy looking down upon him. Closing his eye against the stab of light, he struggled to break from his sleep and into the world of his dreams. Just twenty-four hours ago he was in a makeshift accommodation, his bed under a mosquito net, the air filled with the stench of burnt diesel oil, and the incessant noise of a clapped-out air-conditioning unit drumming in his ears. Now as he looked up at her again as she knelt beside him, her robe draped loosely about her shoulders, saying something about the morning as she leaned forward to kiss him on the cheek. He was not too sure of his answer on the morning, but if this is what Heaven is like he was quite happy to stay there; he slid his hand through the gap in her robe to encircle her waist, and pulled her closer to him. She kissed him on the lips, but checked his emotions with a promise of tomorrow.

"You'd like me to stay over then," he said, giving a broad smile.

"You already know that, my love," she replied with a chuckle, "and before you get too comfortable, my dear, there are a lot of questions to be addressed, such as getting ourselves married."

A little unsure of what he had just heard her say, after the uncertainty to his request the previous evening, Jamie eased her further down upon the bed, and raised himself up enough so that he could look down into those soft brown eyes, as though wanting to read her inner most thoughts. He loved Amy to the end of the world, but in his mind he couldn't see them making this journey without the child, that wouldn't be quite right, he had to know.

"You mean that," he found himself saying, "you really mean that," he added, and without saying another word, Amy confirmed it with a smile, and a nod of her head. She had already thought long and hard as to why she had been given this child, she certainly hadn't asked for it, but she realised it had at last brought Jamie to her door. She was almost thirty-six years old for God's sake – how much longer was she expected to wait for him, they loved one another didn't they? But neither of them seemed to have the courage or the nerve to make the first move, and now she had put it onto his shoulders, and she worried about that. As though seeking the same answers as herself, Jamie laid the palm of his hand across her naval and said, "This little one will be ours, won't it? Truly ours," the tone, and the sincerity of his question almost brought tears to her eyes, for he had given her what she wanted from him, and what she knew was right for them both.

"Yes, darling," she answered, "between us we will give it a life, give it love, and make it our own."

She put her arms around him, and held him tight, telling him how much she loved him, and how she thought this moment would never come, "But," she said, "in this strange way of life we might have to live, our meetings will be as the first, and our love for one another will grow stronger, of that I'm positive."

They breakfasted in their robes, showered, dressed, and put what plans they had into action, and as he had already explained to Amy, their only hope of making it at all possible was with the help of friends. Money was one thing, but the right contacts were even better, so he sat down, and put a call through to both James and Andrew, asking them for their assistance after explaining to them their situation – but not the child, for that knowledge would be theirs and only theirs forever – then giving them Amy's address, with the hope they would be able to meet there in just over an hour's time. This would give him enough leeway to go back to his flat, and return with all the necessary clothes and paperwork required. Whilst there he put a call through to his works site manager, and re-scheduled his flight back until Sunday.

He'd taken a chance in asking his friends to help; he knew that, for with both of their parents in semi-retirement, they were now left with the lion's share of the businesses to run, including the country estates, but the real strength of their friendship was evident when they both arrived within minutes of each other, their faces flushed with excitement and eager to help.

When they sat down, he explained to them the limited time they had in which this marriage could be conducted, and the reasons for it being an informal affair, and on the QT, they agreed to give what help they could, which in fact with the added assistance of their wives, who had already planned to come up to town on Saturday, was more than they had expected.

In under an hour, James had secured a venue for the marriage – a small Oratory to the west of the City, he knew the Minister; time of service 12.30 p.m., and after a bit of persuasion came up with a Registrar, plus James assured them that his wife he knew would be quite happy to provide the buttonholes and a small bouquet. "On top of that," Andrew said, "Lunch at our club, so be there."

After a light lunch which Amy prepared, they headed for the city and the jewellers. He bought her a diamond engagement ring, and a gold wedding ring, at the same time she purchased a ring for him, which they had engraved, and the wedding rings were of course inscribed with the appropriate date, but the engagement ring he had back-dated to the previous year. He also bought her a gold necklace with a pearl drop centre, and matching earrings, whilst she purchased him gold cufflinks, and matching tie-pin. With these essential items in hand they made their way back to the flat to rest before going out to dinner.

After another night of addressing each other's long awaited needs, they awoke to a day of sheer splendour, as one would expect for the last day of May.

This was the day when Jamie Stewart Peterson, Engineering Technician, married Amy Linda Mathem, Playwright, in the company of a small group of friends. It went exactly to plan, and what they'd wished for – photographs were taken, then on to their friends' club for a Champagne lunch.

It was 4 p.m. before they made their final goodbyes, leaving with the usual blessings, and the knowledge that either singly or together they were always welcome to escape from the world by stopping in any one of their country houses – not so much an offer, more of a request.

As they moved towards the entrance doors, the Chef handed Jamie a bag with the bread rolls he'd asked for. From a questioning glance from Andrew he said, "Honeymoon."

"I've got to know more about that, dear boy," Andrew called out as the cab sped away with an overjoyed Amy taking a firm grip upon his arm.

The cab carried them to Hyde Park as he had requested. They got out, and took a stroll along the paths, and down towards the lake, where a number of small children were feeding the ducks. Handing her one of the bread rolls they joined in the fun. "Honeymoon?" she said her face full of laughter.

"Best I can do for now," he replied with a wide grin.

"Couldn't be better," she laughed.

They took a cab back to his flat, this would be her first time there. When they stepped out of the lift onto the landing, he opened his entrance door and lifted her up in his arms, kissed her, and carried her over the threshold.

"Welcome home, my love," he said. "Or at least your other home," he added. He took her hand and guided her around the flat, room by room, including his studio, then brought her back into the lounge, where she stood looking out of the window at the view across the park.

"It's wonderful, darling," she said.

"Thank you," he said, offering her a seat near the piano. "I've spent too many hours alone in this room, sitting here at this piano playing to the girl in that picture," he said, pointing to an enlarged photograph of them at the dance. "And now my love, it was with music you called me, and with the music of love I bless you," and let the piano do the rest of the talking before leaving.

Arriving back at the Bayswater apartments, Amy opened the door to her flat, and turned towards him offering her hand; without hesitating he took it, and in one quick movement lifted her high into his arms as he had done earlier, kissing her warmly on the lips, and once again carrying her over the threshold, pausing just long enough for her to bid him a welcome, before taking her into the lounge, where they fell onto the settee in a heap of laughter. Regaining her breath whilst still holding him to her she said, "I'm still trying to come to terms with all that's happened to us so quickly, Jamie, it all seems surreal."

"I can hardly believe it myself, but if it's a dream don't wake me," he replied.

After having tea, they rested there until late in the afternoon, then showered and dressed for their arranged dinner at the Ritz, altering her hairstyle and make-up a little in the hope of not being recognised, but still looking truly beautiful in a turquoise gown, adding much to the sheen in her chestnut hair, plus the final touch of wearing the gold necklace and earrings he had given her. To Jamie it was one of the proudest moments of his life, entering the foyer of the hotel with his beloved Amy on his arm – that moment would live in his heart forever.

Apart from the resident photographer at the entrance, there were no other intrusions to mar their evening's, enjoyment, and as was expected from a hotel such as the Ritz, the cuisine, wine, and service were excellent, and coupled with the music, to which they danced to, it made the most perfect ending to a wonderful, exciting, extraordinary day.

Returning home well after the midnight hour, the spirit of euphoria still burning within them, they lost no time in slipping between the sheets to hold on to the dream which was now rightly theirs. The desire to satisfy each other's needs was stronger now, but it wasn't, and never would be without thoughts to each other's wellbeing, their love was far deeper than the act.

They awoke late the next morning, reluctant to get up, making every moment of their togetherness count. After a light breakfast, they showered and dressed, and spent what time they had talking, and enjoying each other's company, but as the clock ticked away for him to leave and head back to the Middle East, the conversation became understandably less intense. Neither of them wanted this dream to end, and of all the partings they would have in the future years, this one was the hardest to bear.

He watched her as she packed his, and her wedding gifts into a box that would be placed in the safe, hesitating as she removed her rings from her fingers, turning them over and over in her hand. He put his arm around her and drew her to him, kissing her on the cheek as he saw the tears welling in her eyes.

"You don't have to make this journey, if you so wish, my dear," he said. "You could walk away, and let them find another Linda Fern to make them laugh, cry or whatever, you know that, and at the end of my present contract, I'll be sure to walk with you if that's what you want."

"I know that, my love," she said, her voice hushed, "but there's the child, it has to have a say in this journey, we'll wait for that answer first, and meet each challenge as it arrives, my dearest, all three of us."

Once in the air, Jamie had time to settle down and reflect upon the events of the past forty-eight hours. He might have been on his way to the Middle East, but his heart was still there with Amy, and the totally unexpected fact that in those few short hours, with the aid of his friends, he'd married her, plus she was carrying a child, a child without hesitation for the love of Amy he'd made his own. He'd set his mind on that point, and all the added responsibilities it entailed. He saw Amy's eyes light up when he spoke about it. She knew it would bring changes to both of their lives, but they would be shared, in fact rather than diminish their progress through life; this little speck of light increased it, for responsibility had drive, and it carried them further than they ever dreamed.

It took all the strength of his indomitable character to contain himself when he arrived back at the works compound. The emotional events were still taking their toll, and firing up his veins, and he was struggling to shake them off, but he didn't want to, he wanted to hold on to every precious moment of their time together.

What the hell was he doing out here in this God forsaken hole anyway, his subconscious mind was shouting, and belabouring sorely, and then he knew.

Breathing deeply in this hot, dry, sand-blown air, for some obscure reason he changed from his suit into denims, protective clothing, and hardhat, and strode across the compound and into the site office where a slightly anxious Jim Fieldings, the site manager, was waiting for him.

"Hello, Jim, trouble?" he asked.

"Good to see you back, JP," Jim answered. "Two things at the moment," he said, "firstly the materials are delayed for another two days, and the natives, whoever they are, seem to be spoiling for trouble just to the north of us. I feel we need a lot more security than we already have," he concluded.

"Right," replied Jamie, "I'll round up the powers-that-be in this area, and quietly inform them, no security no refinery."

In the quiet of his cabin he sat down and wrote a nice long letter to Amy. The continuation of their letters to each other was something they had discussed during those wonderful conversations before they parted; it had been their lifeline from the very beginning and there was no reason to stop now, in fact marriage added to the importance of expressing their feelings for each other in a more intimate way than the awkward underlying expressions of the past, even then it all seemed a bit strange, like adding a new dimension to your lifestyle.

All his hopes of returning home within the next two weeks were dashed by the continuous insurgent problems which extended his stay there for a further two weeks. It was not until he had obtained a guarantee from the various government officials, and work on the construction of the plant was well under way, could he send a cable to the office explaining his position. He was given the OK to return home, and take a break for a few days before returning to the office with the final report. With that he left a message on Amy's phone, hoping she was still in the area – after this little lot he needed her more than anything in his life.

He took the afternoon flight home, travelling business class for which the company clients picked up the tab. The extra leg room enabled him to open up his briefcase and complete his final report before he arrived at Heathrow, while everything was still fresh in his mind.

Once into the inner hall of his apartment he placed his coat, holdall, and briefcase in the cloaks cupboard, and checked for messages on his telephone answering machine. Her voice overwhelmed him, "I love you, I love you, I love you, my darling, can't wait until I'm with you again, my love, try to be there – Amy."

"Bless you," he heard himself saying, "I love you.'

With the final rehearsal of the stage play completed, as far as the studio was concerned, any further brush-ups to their lines would now be addressed in Manchester before they opened the following week, which left a delighted Amy almost two days to share with the man in her life.

She'd read his message on the phone pad, and with this break in her working life there was a chance of making the first of his homecomings a little bit special. With her idea firmly fixed in her mind, she headed for the food section of a large department store, making her purchases of both groceries and wine. She returned to her flat just long enough to pick up a small sling bag of necessities, then headed off to Jamie's hoping to be there before him, but it was not to be, though what she saw through the partly open lounge door on that day, placed him before all others in her heart forever.

Jamie followed the usual routine as when returning from these assignments – he quickly stepped out of his clothes, and made for the shower, letting the warmth of the sweet smelling water wipe the slate clean as though the first step into some bright new world, further refreshing himself with a spicy body spray before making his way to the lounge, and his piano, where, clad only in his bathrobe and slip-ons, he could sit down and finally come out of the shadows.

As Amy put the shopping bags down upon the landing floor, in readiness to open the apartment door, she heard the first strains of the piano being played, and realised he'd arrived a little earlier than she'd expected, which without disturbing him meant a slight change of plan to that of welcoming him as he entered the hall. So with the utmost quietness she carefully opened and closed the entrance door behind her, but stopped short of proceeding through the door into the kitchen, to look at him through the partly opened lounge door.

Whilst he was abroad, she'd collected the photograph taken of them at the Ritz, had it enlarged and framed, leaving it on the coffee table as a little surprise gift for when he returned. He'd now placed it in front of him upon the piano, and she knew by the notes that were filling the room, he was pouring his heart out to it. It took all her strength not to run to him, and put her arms around him, but gathering herself up for the task she had planed, she went through and into the kitchen, switched on the oven, set out the table for dinner, opened the wine, prepared the vegetables for the pot, checked on the sweet and put the dishes in the oven that needed cooking. Then, satisfied that all was in order, and that Jamie was still playing the piano, she picked up her sling bag and headed for the shower.

Having prepared well for this, she took the shower cap and toiletries from her sling bag, quickly removed her clothes, and stepped into the shower. Once dry she applied the final touches to her make-up, and wrapped in a large bath towel, she was now ready to meet her man, and for now the rest of the world could wait.

She walked slowly towards him, not wanting to startle him in anyway, intending to move to his side. Jamie was already with her in his thoughts, the face before him lived, and breathed every time his eyes met it, it was when he raised his eyes up once again to search her face, he saw her reflection in the framed glass as she moved closer, lifting his hands high from the keyboard he turned towards her.

"Amy, my love," was all he had time to say before she was in his arms, and lifted high and across his body where her deep sensual kisses were demanding of him, and seeking his arousal, as he on her slipping the knot from the towel to kiss her breasts, then lifting his head to look into her eyes he said, "Now." With a smile of sheer abandonment she said,

"Now." He stood up, still holding her in his arms as the towel fell away, and carried her over to the settee. Lowering her gently down, he slipped off his robe and was with her.

Amy had said their love would grow stronger, at that moment it was all of that, and more so. There was an urgency in their passion for each other, as though they were making it known that every parting demands a redress, and as the climax raced through their bodies they clung holding on to every surge of ecstasy as though it be their last; then, with gentle warm kisses to voice their love, they rested.

They finally dressed and went into the kitchen where they dined on the meal she had prepared for them, and spent a pleasant evening together. He was delighted to know that she would be with him all the following day; so, after breakfast with the morning full of promise for a bright and sunny day, he took her out for a run in his car.

They kept to the country lanes, had lunch in a small village inn, drove down to the coast, and walked hand in hand along the cliff tops like those half their age, visited private gardens and old houses before making their way back, to dine in another inn nearer home. Then, having a nightcap, they enjoyed another night together.

After a little lie-in, they showered, had breakfast, and he drove her back to her apartment. There was sadness, it had been a wonderful two days, and there would be lots more, sometimes even a month, but all priceless.

As Jamie made his way to Fern Bridge to spend the rest of the day with his parents, Amy was on her way to Manchester, and it would be almost two months before they would be able to meet again, spending two more happy days together, using Jamie's flat as a base, which they named The Park, rather than her own flat The Bay, because of the occasional visits from other actors, and scriptwriters – something they would have to address once the child was born.

He was already working on this idea of a number of hideaways where they could relax in peace; they knew the offer was always there from James and Andrew, and having taken Jack Clevedon into his confidence there was a small log cabin in Scotland available to them, plus three friends he'd made abroad. Despite the fact that she was a rising star, she still had a certain amount of freedom.

The next most awkward situation they would have to face in the near future, was to apologise to their parents for keeping their marriage so secret, and of course the child. This they thought they would do when she was five and a half months into her pregnancy. They knew it would be difficult, but at least they were married, and together they could face the world.

They were busy months for both of them. Amy was touring around the country, acting in a series of drama plays, whilst Jamie was in and out of the country. Crossing and re-crossing their paths, desperate for a real break, they wrote their usual letters, spoke over the phone, and snatched a day or two whenever possible, and it was not until mid October before they were given the opportunity to have a week's break, and with it a chance to bring their parents together – something they could delay no longer.

Contacting their parents by phone, coming up with an agreed date, explaining to them that they had matters to discuss and that a car would arrive to pick them up and take them back, went down well. He ordered two cars and drivers from a hire firm, giving them instructions to arrive at the apartment at the same time, after collecting their parents from Fern Bridge, and to assist them to the lift, returning for them at 4 p.m.

They went shopping together, their conversation a little excitable, brought on by the apprehension they felt with the forthcoming meeting of parents, and the reaction to their marriage. They prepared lunch for the family and changed into suitable clothes for the occasion. He wore a dark suit, cream shirt with cufflinks, and blue tie. Feeling pleased, he turned to look at Amy, a new Amy – the pregnancy had brought her into full bloom, and with a plum-coloured cocktail dress, wearing all her jewellery. He'd never seen her look more beautiful, and she saw it in his eyes, and kissed him.

He could hardly wait to see the faces of the parents when they saw her, and when the buzzer sounded at the entrance he nearly jumped out of his skin, then releasing the door catch, they stood holding hands to welcome them, like a couple of teenagers arriving at a party.

As the lift discharged their parents into the waiting arms of their offspring, who quickly ushered them into the apartment, relieving their coats, and seeing them into the lounge, both of them noticed the way the two mothers had taken note of the rings, so once they were seated, having been introduced to each other leaving just Amy and Jamie standing, they came straight to the point of the meeting.

"I think our mothers have already guessed what this meeting was called for," Jamie said.

"And yes, you are right," said Amy, "we are married, and we've asked you all here today to offer our apologies for not informing you of this marriage, or when or where it took place, but I'm sure when you are aware of all that is known about us you will understand. It has been a long courtship, far too long, and love cannot wait forever, less it perish in a veil of tears."

Slowly they laid it all before them – Jamie showed them the letters Amy had written to him since the age of fourteen, and how they had matured over the years, bearing out the sincerity of their love. Amy made everything Jamie said count by adding points of her own, then finally sealing the conversation, by announcing that she was pregnant, and expecting a daughter.

After giving their parents a framed photograph of themselves at the Ritz, plus some pictures of the wedding group, they left them to attend to the lunch, before returning to serve them drinks, and at the same time hoping for a kindly word as to this marriage; they loved them, and didn't want to lose their love.

It was Amy's father, Sir Jacob, who broke the subdued silence by standing up, and walking over to them where he stopped just in front of Jamie, and said, "Jamie Peterson or JP is that correct, young man?"

"That's right, Sir," Jamie replied.

"How strange," added Sir Jacob, "I've heard quite a lot about the antics of JP from my friend Sir Richard who speaks very highly of you, and hopes you're not to be enticed away."

"I doubt that very much, Sir," said Jamie.

"Good," he further added. "On the strength of that, and the friendship between yourself and James and Andrew, whom I also am well acquainted with, plus the love I have for my daughter, I give you my blessing."

"Thank you, Sir," Jamie said as he shook hands with him.

Then, turning to Amy, Sir Jacob said, "You've got yourself a man, little one," and kissed her, and returned to his seat.

Alex stood up, and walked over to the couple as Sir Jacob had. "Remember what I said to you before you went to Glo-Tec, Jamie," he said, "you studied hard, you could have done so many things that you were nothing but a tangle of ideas, and you wanted someone to make you put it altogether, that is exactly why I told you to marry the young lady you were writing to, and let love be your guide, it's stronger than steel." Taking Amy's hand he kissed her on the cheek, and said, "Thank you, young lady, you have my blessing," then turning to Jamie he said, "I'm proud of both of you, take good care of her."

"I will you can be sure of that, Father," Jamie replied.

The two mothers who had been sitting there watching the procedure whilst cradling the framed photographs given to them, suddenly burst out laughing. It was Amy's mother that set them off, with a comment about the menfolk taking the wind out of their sails on the whole affair. Still laughing, they went over and put their arms about the couple to add their own blessings. It was when they said they would be there for them, Jamie said, "I do hope so, Mothers, especially when the little one is born, I would like it to have your love as well as ours."

While the celebration drinks were being poured, and set before their parents, Jamie at Amy's request sat down at the piano, and played them a ten-minute medley of classical music before taking his place and thanking them once again.

The rest of the visit was most enjoyable, with a tour of the apartment, a fine lunch mostly prepared by Amy, and good conversation right up to the time of leaving when they saw them off from the road, and with a promise they would pop down to see them as soon as possible, and most definitely at Christmas.

The next few days passed too quickly for them, and they soon found themselves back in the saddle, working at what seemed harder than ever with little time of their own, but at least they kept the letters flowing.

Although the months seemed long, and the breaks in between so short, before they realised it, it was almost Christmas, which meant shopping in earnest, and quite a new experience as a couple, running in and out of the busy London stores, plus the writing of cards, and wrapping up of presents. It began to dawn on them the wonders of family, and all being well, the following Christmas there would be an extra person around the tree.

Jamie awoke early on Christmas Eve morning, slid quietly out of bed so as not to wake Amy, set the breakfast table, showered, dressed, and made tea, taking it into Amy where he sat and talked to her as they drank it.

They'd been lucky, it was cold, but a fine bright morning whereas other parts of the country had snow, so they quickly threaded their way across London, and on to the M4 taking them west and home; home with his bride – how proud he felt at that moment – home to that fertile valley where both of them had been born. Home to meet the rest of the family – Robert and Sue, Ben and Mary, no longer their little Ben, but a tall ruddy-faced farmer if ever there was one, and Mary was indeed his match, he not only had the farm, but on the other small farm he'd purchased he had a string of horses and ponies and ran a riding stable; he'd made it just as he'd always wanted, and Jamie felt proud of him too.

With just the hum of the tyres on the road Amy too was thinking of this homecoming and the man at her side – what was it her father had said? "You've got yourself a man, little one." She didn't need to be told that as she glanced towards Jamie, this tall broad-shouldered flame-haired man was hers, and she loved him with all her heart, and now he was taking her home. She thought about her home where she was born, high on the hillside from where she could look down at Fern Bridge and its river which flowed gently along to the sea. She loved the town, and its quietly spoken people, and the view across to the distant hills which in the autumn were a blaze of colour. She'd always wanted to walk there, and now with Jamie at her side they could take their daughter to see its beauty. Letting her thoughts run faster, she put her hand on his thigh, and squeezed it, he lowered his hand on top of hers to do likewise, and said, "I love you dearly."

"Me too," she said.

Arriving at No.20 Mill Drive to find a host of excited faces already waiting for them, he doubted Amy had ever seen so many willing hands to help them with their coats, and hats, or rushing around to provide them with a warming cup of tea. She felt a little overwhelmed by it all, but having been introduced to each and every one of them, and listened to their chatter over lunch, she began to feel the warmth that ran through this family's life, something she'd never known, and she loved it.

As they made their final goodbyes, Jamie heard her quietly asking his mother if she could pop in to see her when she came this way again; he never had any worry over his family, if he had Amy had eradicated it.

He stopped the car just before turning into the main drive of Fern Manor, looking across at Amy he said, "Are you all right, dear, they didn't make you too tired did they? They were all a bit excitable."

"I'm fine," she said, "I'm sure we'll get plenty of rest once we're here, and by the way we have an old retainer by the name of Albert – he will take the cases in – he should have retired years ago, but sees no reason to, so Father keeps him on."

Stopping in front of the main entrance steps, Jamie released the boot, got out of the car, and went around to help Amy just as a little grey-haired gentleman appeared as if from nowhere. "Welcome home, Miss Amy," he said. Amy put her arms around him, and kissed him saying, "Oh thank you, Albert, please come and meet my Jamie."

"Nice to meet you, Albert," Jamie said, holding out his hand.

"And you, Sir," he said, taking his hand. "I'll see to the cases, you run along up – Lady Vivian is waiting for you."

Taking just the two small parcels, and his arm firmly locked into hers, they mounted the steps to the entrance, where before entering he took a quick look back over Fern

Bridge and thinking how strange it all seemed. What was it his Grandfather said? "Life's all heads and tails, lad."

They entered to be warmly greeted by her parents, but before he knew what was happening Amy was spirited away by two overdressed old biddies, and swept into the drawing room with what looked like a sign of despair on her face, whilst he was slapped on the back by their menfolk, and more or less bundled into Sir Jacob's den, by someone calling him old chappie and handing him a whisky, where these two jokers proceeded to bore him and Sir Jacob with a lot of nonsensical prattle, until the call came to dress for dinner when they made their escape.

Amy looked to have suffered the same fate when he met her in the bedroom, except for giving him a quick hug and kiss. She looked decidedly a little subdued, and there was no doubt knowing Amy he would hear about it in due course.

He wasn't sure who arranged the dinner seating, but he was positive it wasn't exactly how Lady Vivian had planned it, for he found himself cut out once again by these two charmers, who had hardly said a word to him since he'd arrived.

It made the whole of the dinner, and even the coffee and brandy taken in the drawing room, a laboured affair. Whatever Amy was feeling was anyone's guess; but for himself, caught as he was between these two dear old chappies, he felt his brain was going numb, and he gave a silent sigh of relief when Amy said she thought Jamie and herself should retire, having had a very long day.

They stood up, bid their goodnights, and made their way to the foot of the stairs where they paused and, without a spoken word, turned and hugged each other before quickly mounting the stairs and into their bedroom to escape for the night.

As he closed the curtains, and turned back the bed-sheets on the large four poster, Amy went into the dressing room, changed into her nightdress, and proceeded into the en suite, a procedure carried out in complete silence and which he also followed. He was surprised on coming out of the suite to find the bedroom in darkness, except for a faint glimmer of light from the partly opened curtains – light that arose from the distant street lamps and Fern Bridge.

The same light picked her out from the shadows as she stood there looking out into the night, and as he approached her he heard in the stillness of the moment the faint sound of her spoken thoughts into the night, what sounded like real people being voiced almost in a whisper from her, though unsure.

He put his arm around her waist, and they stood there together looking out at Fern Bridge with its twinkling Christmas lights and a glint of silver as the lights on the bridge caught the river's flow. So many times she must have stood there completely alone, but now it was their room, and they could share the view together as long as it was possible.

She reached out to open a small side window, letting the cold night air sweep in. He pulled her closer to him saying, "You'll catch a cold, my love." She turned to look up at him, and it was then he saw the tears that lay in her eyes. Drawing her even closer, he placed a gentle kiss upon her lips, and said, "This wont do, my love, we can't have the little one hear you cry," as a hint of a smile creased her lips. He closed the sash, and led her over to the bed, switching on the bedside light, and seeing her safely between the sheets before closing the curtains, and joining her, where he lay for a few moments looking into those dewy soft brown eyes, and saying, "I think we should talk a little before we snuggle down, my love, don't you? She nodded to confirm his request.

She took his hand, cupped it in both of hers, pressing it to her as she listened to him, even though the conversation was of the upsetting events of the day, his voice filled her, and excited her as she to him.

"I thought I'd lost you forever to those terrible people my love, and I'm sure they're not relatives, but whoever they are your father was none too impressed with them, and I'm sure he was hoping that the young Jamie of old didn't rise up like Phoenix from the ashes, and throw them out, but I have too much respect for him. Furthermore, my dear," he added, "Who were those real people you mentioned looking lost – Robert, Sue, or Ben and Mary?"

Amy lay there listening to him, her smile broadening by the minute, until finally she spoke of those inner thoughts she had voiced.

"Yes, through the downbeat experience we have had during the latter part of this day, my dear," she said, "I most certainly was thinking about those happy folks down there, especially Ben and Mary – they truly are real people. The four strangers you met here today are false, like cardboard cut-outs, and not relatives in any shape or form. They are offshoot figures of long past business connections, and feel they have a right to invite themselves into various homes, and functions. Father is too polite to refuse, so we have to suffer them for another day, my darling," she added.

"I had a feeling they were trying to split us up," he said.

"Bit late for that, dear," she replied, "you see one of the dear ladies there brought her son, a junior MP, here several times, hoping for a match. It was not only that I didn't like him but in my heart, as you full well know, I was already engaged to you," she chuckled; the clouds which had creased her brow were lifting now, and when he spoke of speaking to her mother over the seating arrangements, or talking to the ladies themselves, the real Amy was fast returning, "diplomatically I hope."

"Of course," he replied.

"Of this I have to see," she added.

"Coming from a young engineer who stuck a hardhat on an interfering Minister of Trade's head, and said, 'If you know more about this construction than I do, then you'd better get on with it while I have a cuppa with the lads'." The explosion of laughter came as he knew it would, and with it they rocked themselves to sleep, fully armed to fight another day.

After a welcome cup of tea in bed, brought in by Mrs Page the housekeeper, they dressed and went down to breakfast, waving aside one of the ladies' suggestions as to where Amy should sit, by going around the table Jamie made sure she was seated between her mother and himself as he had suggested – much to the dismay of those who had thought otherwise.

It all went along quite well, with a certain amount of chatter, but when one of the ladies broached the subject of what to do after breakfast, Jamie stopped her in her track by announcing that he and Amy were going to church.

"Are we all driving?" she asked.

"No," Jamie replied, "we're walking to All Saint's Church, in Purple Brow, about two miles up the hill." Upon that statement there was a measured silence, until she said, "Oh in that case we'll just read a bit until you get back."

As they made their way up to their dressing room for warm clothing she said, "What a good idea, where did that come from?"

"Some diplomat I know," he replied with a grin.

"You devil," she chuckled, "but I like it."

They'd no sooner dressed, and made their way onto the front drive when they were called to a halt by Amy's mother wishing to join them. "Another escapee," Jamie said, as they linked arms, and strode up the hill together. The conversation was light-hearted and warming, and he suspected that at that moment mother and daughter were closer than they had ever been – they had a lot of making up to do.

The church at Purple Brow was built mainly from the outcrop of colourful rock which gave the small hamlet its name, offering a service to several other villages along the rest of this hillside. Jamie had attended here on various occasions during his youth, and could not imagine anyone there today who would recognize him, but he was very wrong, and in a lot of ways happy about it.

Still walking side by side as they passed under the lychgate, they were confronted by the Reverend Speers who greeted Lady Vivian and Amy warmly before turning to Jamie to take his hand. As he looked up at Jamie the recognition came back to him. "Good Lord, it's Jamie isn't it? Jamie Peterson," he said.

"That's right, Sir," he said, "I thought you had long retired."

"Not yet, young man" he added, then looking at Amy and Jamie he said, "come and see me after coffee."

The three of them left the vicinity of the church, linked together as before, almost skipping down the hill with Jamie in the centre. Whether it was that little church, the service, carols, children with their gifts, or the fact finding conversation with the Reverend Speers, they held on to each other perhaps a little tighter, with a determination to make this first Christmas together come alive.

They arrived back in time to dress for Christmas lunch, which would be the main meal of that day, the evening meal being a cold buffet, to which Jamie had suggested Amy and himself would bring it in from the kitchen, having sent the staff home, or off duty after lunch, and to his delight Lady Vivian fell in with the idea.

There were no further attempts to interfere with the seating arrangements, leaving them all to enjoy an excellent lunch in a more sociable atmosphere at the end of which, having taken their coffee and brandy in the drawing room, Jamie made sure Amy went off to rest, whilst he settled down in a large armchair with a book.

Amy's parents seemed quite happy for Jamie to take command, so after the Queen's speech, assisted by the two remaining staff that steadfastly refused to leave (Albert and

Mrs Page), he organized the tea, and at the same time requested that these two old retainers should join them for the evening, a request that found favour in Sir Jacob's camp.

Whatever the troublesome four had in mind he was not too sure, or even cared any more; he'd planned out the evening, and it was up to them to join in, and this came immediately after the buffet when he sat down at the piano, playing a number of classics, and modern compositions, accompanied either by Amy or her mother whose trained voices filled the air and brought a lot of pleasure he knew to Sir Jacob himself, finally concluding at 11 p.m. By half past the hour, both Amy and himself were snuggled down, and fast asleep.

By 10 a.m. the following morning with the visitors long gone, they were at last free to sit and chat amongst themselves. The phone rang and Amy picked it up. Watching her from where he was seated, he saw the surprised look, and the flood of delight that filled her already smiling face.

"Mary!" she exclaimed, "how nice to hear from you, what do we owe this honour to?" Between the occasional breaks in the conversation he heard her say, "We'd love to, I'm sure my parents will be quite happy to travel on it," and "it's all very romantic," and then "I'll break the news to him, and let him ring you back."

Walking over to sit alongside of him she said, "That was Mary, my love, and she kindly invited us to lunch tomorrow."

"I'm really pleased about that," he said, "not only because I know you enjoy her company, but to see her kitchen where we'll eat – and you need to see it to believe it – it's an industry!" he chuckled. "What's all this romantic bit you were discussing?" he added.

"Ben bought a surrey early in the year, it's now really beautiful," she said, "after Ben and Robert have worked on it. He wants to bring it up to the Manor by 9 a.m. tomorrow, for you to drive us all down to the farm via The Folds, which he said is the scenic route, and you know it well," she finally added.

"I'll kill him," he said through a fit of laughter, "but for you, my love, I'll drive the thing, and it could be very pleasant indeed."

Ben arrived right on time with a grin as wide as the sky, his own horse attached to a long halter at the rear. "Good morning, good people," he said, "your chariot awaits."

With the help of foldaway steps Roberts had designed, both Amy and her parents were able to quickly gain their seats, with plenty of travel rugs around them, and given the final instructions from Ben, Jamie got underway.

Once they had made the initial climb to Purple Brow, and turned left, the route along the crest of the hill was more or less on a level plane, and the views on either side were beautiful even at this time in the year.

The road went straight through three villages on the route, each one no more than a mile and a half apart – Sold Fold, Midden Fold, and Nor Fold – and what pleased them greatly was the cheery welcome they received from the locals as they passed by. Amy turned to look over her shoulder at her parents – they were snuggled up close as she was to Jamie – and by their faces thoroughly enjoying every moment of it. Pulling herself even closer to Jamie, she lifted her face towards him for a kiss, and received it with pleasure.

He turned off the main carriageway at the Bleak Barn, to take the long easy gradient known as Keepers Lane, down to the valley floor, where they crossed the river via Drakes Ford and where the river waters were almost up to the wheel hubs, turning south which would take them back towards Fern Bridge, and the farm. Their first stop was at the Drakes Bell Inn where Daniel, under the orders of Ben, was waiting for them with a welcome mug of coffee. Once refreshed they soon got underway, and reached the farm at half past twelve in the afternoon, as Ben had said they should do, to be further welcomed by a happy smiling Mary who quickly ushered them into the warmth of the farmhouse.

Jamie stood back a little, waiting for their reactions when they finally entered Mary's kitchen. Even from where he stood just outside, the smell of freshly baked bread, cured ham, herbs and spices were making great demands upon his palate, drawing him quickly inside to where the others were gazing around in amazement at all the shelves full of various types of preserved food, from jams to fruit and vegetables, and some like herbs suspended from the ceiling, kept comfortably warm by a double Aga. In the centre was a large well-scrubbed pine kitchen table with a number of rush place mats upon it, and to one end an equally large gammon was sat waiting to be carved, and set out on the plates by its side. Jamie took Amy's hand, giving it a little squeeze he said, "You alright my love?"

"More than alright, dear," she said. "In fact standing here I feel really wonderful."

They were joined in the kitchen by the three children – Graham the eldest, Sally, and five-year-old Pete. As soon as they were all seated they were served with their lunch which was gammon, mashed potatoes flavoured with chives, green string beans (though from Mary's preserves they tasted like freshly picked ones) and carrots, freshly baked bread, farm butter, and a selection of pickles and chutney. The final touch being a glass of home-brewed ale, and fruit-flavoured water for the three youngsters. Jamie was justly proud of his brother, and all he and Mary had achieved, but never more than at that moment when he stood there embracing the true farming tradition, and said grace, before lifting his glass and wishing one and all a very happy New Year.

Mary's apple pie completed the meal, but not the conversation which became split into two separate themes for discussion – on the one hand there were Graham, Ben and Sir Jacob who was very impressed with Ben and Mary's achievements, buying the market garden to the south, creating riding stables to the north, and incorporating them into one unit as Home Farm with the help of ten employees.

On the other side of him Jamie had Amy and her mother with Mary and Sally, whose conversation ran as usual from the household matters to children, including the day of their birth, leaving Jamie happily and quite content with young Pete in the middle. Twice Amy turned to look at him, giving his leg a squeeze, bringing a chuckle from her mother who spotted it. As for Pete, who had moved closer to Jamie sitting next to his favourite uncle, life couldn't be better; he'd told all his classmates about him, how his uncle went into the jungle to help the people trapped there, and when the cannibals saw him wearing that white hat they all fled – yes for Pete it was a great morning.

Arriving back at the Manor, Amy took Jamie's advice and went up to rest, her mother nodding to him said, "I'll do the same, young man, and no doubt Sir Jacob and yourself will do likewise." As it was, Sir Jacob was already ahead on those lines.

"Come into the study, my boy," he said, "we'll have a little something before we lay back, and do a bit of thinking," the same thinking overcame Jamie as he sought the comfort of a large armchair.

The last few days at the Manor before returning to London were amongst the happiest they would have there, if it was indeed possible. The four of them seemed to be closer than ever, no doubt due to the subdued excitement of the coming child, which was now at times kicking lively within Amy.

Meal times grouped together at one end of the long dining room table was also an enjoyable affair, with plenty of chatter. They went out during those cold crisp mornings, mother and daughter, their arms linked together, slightly ahead of Jamie and Sir Jacob – a most unusual exercise for the old gentleman to undertake nowadays, but for the time being he seemed to be enjoying it. Jamie liked his company, especially his conversation, he'd grown fond of the old gentleman, and in those discussions they'd learnt quite a lot about each other and gained from them. Sir Jacob quickly realized what an intelligent son-in-law he had, and where he was heading in life. On his side Jamie was given a clearer insight into the world of commerce and finance than he had ever known, a knowledge which would add to both Amy and his daughter's future.

New Year's Eve saw them well wrapped up standing just outside the main entrance doors, accompanied by Albert and Mrs Page, drinks in hand, listening for the church bells down there in Fern Bridge to strike midnight, then with glasses raised they toasted the new year, and embraced with love in their hearts.

Although Amy could have stopped at the Manor until the baby was born she steadfastly refused, wanting to be as close to Jamie as possible. They'd made this choice, and they would stand by it together, so two days into the new year he drove them back to London, stopping at The Park for a further two days, and from there Amy decided to return to The Bay for at least another two weeks before rejoining Jamie at The Park.

Amy went back to the studio the following day, and with the aid of clever photography canned the rest of the short play they had produced, signed off, and went back to The Bay to copy out a series of scripts she'd been working on, at the same time informing Jamie of her whereabouts.

Jamie set off to the main office almost at the same time as Amy. After bidding all those he met a happy new year, he quickly settled down in his office to check over the in-tray, and by 11 a.m. he was in full flow, when from a tap on the door Jane appeared, with a smile that had more than a hint of mischief about it. "Good morning, Sir," she said, "A very happy new year to you, and yours," she added lightly touching the top of the picture frame. "Trust they're all well?"

"Quite well," Jamie said. "And a happy new year to you, Jane. To what do we owe this visit to?" he added.

"Sir Richard would like a word or two with you, Sir, if that's alright."

"Right, Jane," he said, signing the paper he had in his hand, and on dropping it into the out-tray, followed her out of the office.

Sir Richard stood up when Jamie entered his office, walked around his desk, and shook hands with him wishing him a happy new year, then offering him a seat.

"Firstly I felt it's about time that I congratulated you on your marriage to Miss Amy, whom I've known for a very long time, being a friend of her father Sir Jacob. Of course I recognized her in that photograph you have on your desk, but never in my widest dreams could I ever imagine you were that close. I thought it was just a one-off at whatever dance you were invited to, and I must say I'm very happy for you both, and I also know Sir Jacob is very impressed with you from the conversations you had together over the Christmas period," he said, "and it's to the questions he put to you as to your position within this company, as regards to your long-term future, with thoughts to his daughter, and her expected child, that I made the situation or the road forward to you as clear as possible, and I hope you will take it on," he further added.

Looking across his desk at Jamie he said, "I've been given to understand that by this time next year I will be promoted to consultant, and a member of the Board, my seat here will by taken by Mr Jack Clevedon, and it has been suggested that you take over his office – that's of course if you still want to remain with us, and I for one hope you do," he added.

At that Jamie nodded, for in his own field of play his mind and soul was firmly focussed on Amy and the child. "Mr Clevedon," he continued, "will hold this post for a further three to four years when he wishes to retire to that Swedish chalet he has constructed in the Grampians, upon which time this office, and your position within the company will be secure, and the way open right up to the Board if you so wish."

Jamie stood up, and offered his hand to Sir Richard and said, "Thank you for that, Sir, and thank you for having so much faith in me from the very beginning."

Sir Richard laughed at that, and said, "You're made for a company such as this, JP, and I remember telling the Board that they could not afford to let you go, and the same applies today." With that Jamie left to find Jane waiting for him.

Trying to put a glum expression on his face he said, "I'm leaving."

"You most certainly are, Sir," she replied, seeing right through him. The day after tomorrow we're sending you across the channel for two days to kick a few backsides, then you can tell me a little more about all these stories I keep hearing." With that she reached up, and kissed him on both cheeks saying, "Congratulations, Sir, I'm very pleased for you, and of course I would hope to meet the young lady at some future date."

"For you, Jane, that's a certainty," he replied.

"Before you go back to your office I must introduce you to Mr John Wilkes our new engineer who will be taking over your office when you move," Jane said. "He is not new to the job, having worked for other companies, but needs to be groomed into our way of operating, which would be a part of your duties over the coming months," she added, "and I believe they're looking for another one to keep you busy," she laughed.

"How kind of you," he said, quickly slipping back into his office, and shutting the door.

Amy returned to The Park during the third week in January to wait there until it was time for the birth of the child. Jamie also took leave, and like Amy bringing enough paperwork to keep them busy. They already had the cot there, and most things needed for the new arrival, so this waiting time had to be filled in whatever way they could for the weather was pure January.

Keeping themselves occupied during the daytime and into the evenings was never any problem for their love of general conversation was endless, but the nights never seemed to fold so easily into place. Amy, like any expectant mother for the first time, even with all the exercises and ante-natal care, knew there could still be problems, but the scan results were good, and she knew it was a girl, but what else? It gave her plenty to think about. It was all like some strange journey – she didn't want to remember the very beginning, she could have terminated this little mite, but something even through her anger was holding her. By God she was angry, then through the clouds of shattered dreams Jamie was there, he was her dream, he asked questions until her anger fell upon him. Why did she do that, she'd asked herself, he could have told her to go to hell, but he told her he loved her. She smiled, she took him to her bed, he was beautiful, so beautiful, and always placing her needs first, a gentle gentleman. Then there was Christmas, and Mary – she liked her a lot, so well organized, and that surrey with her parents sitting there looking so contented and with the steady clop of the horses hoofs still firmly in her mind. She could easily recall lifting her face up into the cool crisp light for the warmth of Jamie's loving kiss to hold hers. With a smile upon her lips she moved a little closer, felt the warmth of his body run through her, and slept.

A little after midnight on the 10th of February Amy awoke Jamie with the news that her labour pains had started. Having all the necessary items packed and ready, they were safely in the maternity clinic within twenty minutes, where he was ushered into a small side room to await until the birth was imminent, and at that point he would be allowed in to be with her at the birth.

It was a slow painful journey for Amy, taking almost five hours. During the last hour Jamie was with her, wiping her brow, and working the gas and air as instructed, and when the little one finally made its way into the world, he could but marvel by what he'd seen. Taking Amy's hand to his lips he kissed it and said, "It's over now, my love." She nodded, not ready to speak and plainly very tired.

He watched as the doctor and nurses busied themselves around her, raising her up with extra pillows, and finally the moment arrived with the midwife placing the baby into her arms.

"You've a beautiful healthy daughter, Mrs Peterson," she said. Like Amy, Jamie looked down at this mite, and was almost speechless in wonder, it was practically like a carbon copy of Amy, complete with her chestnut hair. Jamie was lost for words when the young nurse spoke to him, the joy he felt at that moment was overwhelming.

"Your eyes," she said, "Your daughter has your blue eyes, Sir," Amy heard it too, pulled him towards her, and kissed him.

"We were right, we were so right, Jamie my love, it's ours."

With the child now fed, and placed in its cot after Jamie had cradled her in his arms, hardly daring to move or breathe for fear of this dream collapsing into nothingness, Amy settled down in the bed to rest, though first telling Jamie to go home and do likewise, for he would be back there at 4 p.m. when they would have the joy of telephoning their folks with the news. As he stood at the door to blow her a kiss, she said, "Now go home, and rest, and I mean rest, Mr Peterson."

"Will do," he replied not sure if he could ever sleep again.

He entered his flat, picked up the mail from the mat, and tossed it onto the hall table, before removing his coat and jacket, and walking into the lounge where he drew back the curtains. He looked down at the park where the sun's lowly rays were struggling to do the same, gliding amongst the trees' garland of frost, turning it into a winter wonderland. His eyes were now full of tears as he wept unashamedly, and through the mist of tears he looked up at the sky, and said, "Thank you, God, for Amy, and this child, thank you, thank you," and wept on until drained of tears to prepare to rest.

Jamie arrived back at the clinic with a spring in his step, an arm full of flowers and goodies and a smile as wide as the sky, to see Amy waiting for him, arms outstretched to embrace him, and smother him with kisses. This was one happy man! And to Jamie the most wonderful woman in the world.

Shortly after tea and cake brought into them by a young nurse, Amy put a call through to her mother giving her the glad news, and from the look on Amy's face, the excitement on the other end was beyond words, and by the time they had finished talking to both sets of parents they were exhausted, but very happy.

Jamie's suggestion of sending a car to bring them all up on the following day was waived by Sir Jacob who insisted he would do the honours by hiring a car from Fern Bridge. "Once we have paid our respects to you all, dear boy, I'll take our little party off to my club for lunch," he said. As for our valiant two they were delighted, leaving them only to enquire if they may have coffee in the room for their parents.

No doubt starting off early they arrived almost on the dot of 11 a.m., their faces flushed with excitement at the prospect of seeing this new addition to the family. As for their daughter, Jamie could already see the changes that were occurring in just twenty hours – her skin was becoming lighter and less wrinkled, but when each of the grandmothers took turns in holding her, he was taken aback when she opened her eyes to look up at them. Perhaps it was the sound of new voices, but whatever it was certainly made their visit even more pleasurable, and a knowing smile and nod to him from Amy found his heart, and danced with it.

When the question of names arose Jamie left it to Amy to explain what they had decided upon, and why. Taking Jamie's hand she said, "We have given much thought to what names we should impose on our little one, for she has to live with them. We wanted names that we thought sounded right to her, and meant something to us all," she continued. "We also wanted to use your initials, for you have given us so many abilities and with that in mind her first name will be Verlisity, and the second for thoughts of future years, Jessica."

"God is looking," Jenna said, Amy nodded, her mother stood up, went over to them, and kissed them saying, "they're beautiful, just beautiful, I love you both."

In the short two hours the little party were there, much was made over their future arrangements as regarding their work, and the child's welfare, and to this they assured them that nothing was being taken lightly. Yes they would press on with their chosen careers, but Verlisity would always be the prime mover in their thoughts, and the way ahead. Jamie's words over their commitments were a challenge.

"There had to be a way for us, and the little one there has to be." They'd taken up that challenge, and love was the sword, as it always has been throughout the ages.

It was Amy who presented them with their way forward, leaving Jamie to slip in any comments that he found necessary. She explained that she did not intend to go back to the studio for at least six months and then only to check on what possible parts she may be asked to play next year.

Between that they were hoping to fix a date with the Reverend Speers with the view of having Verlisity christened at All Saints Purple Brow this June or early July. He saw the delight in their faces to that statement, and she also explained they might make it down there in the autumn, but would be sure to be there for Christmas.

Slowly but surely they set out the plans they had made for themselves and Verlisity, plans that would allow Jamie to reach the most senior position within his company, and for her to climb to the heights of her profession without in anyway jeopardizing the love and trust of their child. "For Verlisity," Amy said, "we would walk away from it all."

"Finally," Amy said, "we'd like our two talented mothers to teach her in the love of art and music, the very soul of life, we don't want her to be an actress or an engineer, but with hope just keep her feet firmly on the ground, and one day find a good partner who will do the same."

Amy returned to The Park with Verlisity after the fourth day. Jamie was also with them over the following few weeks, having had work sent to him from the office, something they'd agreed to do, and collecting it when completed until he gradually made his way back into the office.

They would have many good or special years in their marriage, but this was their first real year as a family, a year in which mother and daughter, and Jamie as her father bonded together, a year when Verlisity would meet her extended family, be christened at Purple Brow, and feel the warmth of those around her. And in the autumn, to be held in her mother's arms, for her mother to direct the gaze of those deep blue eyes to the distant wooded hills, now ablaze with autumn's shimmering glory, and to spend her first Christmas under the loving gaze of her grandparents with the equally happy faces of Albert and Mrs Page at their side. And when her parents stood on those steps again, to bless in another new year, she was safely in the land of nod with all she'd seen and heard carefully tucked away in a corner of her tiny mind, to enjoy on a cloudy day.

With dogged determination, our couple of destiny moved ever towards where at some point they would reach the pinnacle of their chosen professions, after working their way through life's bright or shadowed uncertain paths, where the strain of those partings to further their aims, and the sheer rapture of those homecomings, reclaiming the love that bound them in union with the child they had made their own, to blend in a pattern of dreams.

It was with a great deal of pride when Jamie took over Sir Richard's office from the retiring Jack Clevedon, and it was Sir Richard himself who offered him his chair, but it was not only he who was on the move, for there were already signs of a move within the company itself, as with the rest of the world at large, in a drive for expansion, the type of which Glo-Tec were world leaders.

During his reign in the London office from where he followed Sir Richard's example as one of the consultant directors in the Board Room, after having received a knighthood at the age of fifty-eight for work on crown properties, the London-based side of the company more than trebled in size and operations, with a vast amount of contracts on the books assuring him a permanent position on the Board.

With the help of a Nanny plus Verlisity's entry into a kindergarten at the age of two, Amy slowly began to make her way back into her career of script-writing short one-off plays for TV, and feature films made almost entirely in the studio, but as time progressed it became necessary to go out on locations further afield – something she had to endure though she hated it as it brought back too many bad memories. The separation from both Jamie and Verlisity was at the best of times hard to bear.

It was during her fiftieth year when she spent the longest period away from them – three months filming in the States; she almost walked away, but with Jamie and Verlisity encouraging her, and promising to keep those letters and phone calls flowing, she made the journey which brought her fully into the spotlight and onto the big red carpet of the award ceremonies, and finally being made a Dame for her performing art. These were precious moments, not only for her mother who'd set her on this course, but Jamie whose love and patience was endless.

The dark shadows that crossed their paths during the fifth, and sixth years of their marriage were the deaths of the two fathers. Alex finally succumbed to his war wounds, and in Sir Jacob's case it was the question of age. For Verlisity the pain was in the disbelief that these kindly grandfathers were going away, and she would never see them again, Alex had sung to her, and Sir Jacob had read stories to her. For Amy, Alex's loss was a man with a merry twinkle in his eyes, and a soft Scottish burr, full of down-to-earth wisdom, and akin to her own father in many ways and who she loved dearly. For Jamie, Alex was his rock, the man who had made him a man of steel, and was always there for him with advice and encouragement. Sir Jacob added to all he'd become, to polish his act with a few extra words of wisdom to make him a man of substance.

Verlisity, this little dark-haired blue-eyed spark of life, had an impish smile that held you, daring you to laugh, and when you did so collapsing in fits of laughter revelling in her own conquest. She was a loveable, happy child, and like most others when at that tender age, full of little surprises, the most noticeable of these was her protectiveness towards them, something she clung to all her life. It was uncanny at times, as though when she was just a thought in her mother's womb, she'd heard every word they'd said about her, and the pledge they'd made to give her life, and love, and for that she seemed to be making them hers, rather than vice versa.

The evening when Amy walked down the red carpet at the BAFTA awards, looking stunningly beautiful, a young actor put his arm around her, and kissed her on the cheek to please the waiting crowd, Verlisity sitting at the table with him, squeezed his arm, and said, "It's only pretending, Daddy."

Looking down at her he said, "You know it, and I know it, but they don't do they?' She broke into a giggle, adding a long "Noooo." It was exactly the same when Jamie had to preside at an opening ceremony, surrounded by elegantly dressed young ladies, leaving Amy to assure her that he was theirs.

At her own engagement party he casually said to her, "So it looks like we're going to lose you, little one." She looked up at him saying, "That will never ever happen, Father, and you know that, I'll always be near, and only God can prove me wrong." There was a lump in his throat that day when he answered, and kissed her on the cheek, "I guess so my love, I guess so."

As they moved into the sixtieth years of their life's journey, the shadowy pages crossed their path once again with the loss of their dear mothers, slipping away within eighteen months of each other, almost in the same divided way as their fathers so many years past.

These talented ladies, whose friendship towards each other had blossomed over the many years since the death of their loved ones, would be sadly missed. Even though their frailty had somehow found them wanting with the events of each day, they had contributed so much towards the family's wellbeing, and had been the very backbone to our couple's success, easing their journey with the valuable assistance they had given towards Verlisity's progress in life, right from an early age, leading her into the world of art and music as they'd hoped they would do. But behind the sadness of their loss that lay deep within their hearts, there was also an element of joy – joy in remembering the glow in their faces when they took turns in holding Verlisity at her birth, joy as she aspired at the business college to obtain her degree, joy at her wedding to Johnathan Percival, and again holding her firstborn. There were also those extra special events, when they went to the Palace with them, to see the Queen present them with the honours they had so rightly earned.

The void they experienced when Verlisity left home after her marriage, though she was never that far away, appeared to grow larger with the loss of their dear mothers, and a sense of emptiness crept into their lives, and they knew then it was time to stop, and make the rest of the journey together.

As Jamie stood at the window, looking down at the Park bathed in early morning spring sunshine, he was joined there by Amy who slid her arm around him. They loved this flat, and its view, and intended to keep it as long as they needed it. She'd sold The Bay some years ago, and they had a small place in the country, but this apartment had special memories that would live on. Though today they had other things on their minds – today was the day when they would put their plans in motion to walk away from it all, and Jamie was about to make a start this morning after which he would only be there for presentations, and the AGMs.

In the time that followed, Amy went up to Cumbria to complete the work in a film she'd been making as a director, whilst Jamie liaised between the office and the Board Room over the many discussions and problems that filled every minute of his day.

At 10.30 a.m. on the 6th of June, the balding grey-haired figure of Maxwell Rulberge flashed his ID card at the doorman, and made his way into the City Central TV Studios, then with a quick word with the receptionist headed for one of the recording studios. Quietly opening the door, he stepped inside shutting it behind him, and waited before taking another step to allow his eyes to adjust to the subdued lighting.

It was then he saw the one he'd come to meet – Amy, or to him Linda Fern, for he'd been her agent for many years, and on hearing her future plans he'd come to convey both his and his wife's best wishes for the road ahead.

She had her back towards him working on the monitor, checking out the short film to which she'd been the director, and he guessed this one would be her last, unless of course she changed her mind, and he very much doubted that. She'd discarded her beige jacket, and stood there on light-tan leather shoes with medium-sized heels, wearing pale pink jeans and a cream top, her hair now white still danced in flowing locks around her neckline, and he could but marvel at her neat trim figure. He knew that even at her present age she could still dance the night away. He not only admired her, he loved her, she was a true professional.

He cast his mind back to when Verlisity was just a small child, a child that had brought her beauty out into full bloom. He thought of the young actors half her age seeking her favours, but there were none forthcoming; the senior star members of the cast on locations hoping to share her bed, as many a young starlet might have done so. But with Linda he knew there was never a chance, she had her man, and held him high in her heart, and that's why he loved her. He had a great liking for Jamie, he liked his musical talent, his sparkling deep blue eyes, his head of fire – given a chance he knew he could have put his name up there in lights, but he also knew that taking Jamie away from the profession he loved would destroy him. He took them to dinner at the Savoy with his wife Emma, and as they watched the magic of their dancing, he found Emma tugging at his sleeve, "What's it with them, Maxie," she said, "are they drinking the same wine as we are? So maybe you tell me it's love, but it's deeper than that, Maxie, something is holding them, and you should know, are you not her agent?" But he didn't and doubted if he ever would.

He walked over, and greeted her, kissing her on both cheeks. She repeated the warmth of its meaning and said, "It's good to see you, Max."

"And you," he replied, "I'll miss you, you know."

"Not so, Max," she answered, "we'll be there at the ceremonies, and the Charity Do's, and there's always the odd dinner dates." He nodded. "Anyway," she continued, "Why don't you do the same as Jamie and myself, and call it a day, then you could take Emma to St. Petersburg and show her where you were born."

With that he burst out laughing, almost collapsing, "My Emma," he said, "going out of London," shaking his head, "she really believes that anywhere south of Croydon or north of Enfield is a jungle, and the people out there will eat you alive." He kissed Amy once more on the cheeks and left saying, "See you around, my pet, take care," and walked, still laughing, out of the door.

That morning also found Jamie with plenty to think about. He'd just arrived back from Europe where he'd been to represent the company at the opening of two vast shopping complexes – he hated them with their spires and domes, relating them to aircraft hangers with bowler hats, but if this is really what the general public wanted, then so be it. At least the local authorities in the Fern Valley had avoided such a disaster, promoting one twenty-five miles to the north well clear of the area. This always made Christmas in particular a little special to them when going down to see the family, the small shops ablaze with Christmas lights, and the tree in the square welcoming them every time they went there, and in so many ways making their eventual return a certainty.

As soon as he entered the Board Room that morning he knew it was going to be a little bit special, not because of the paperwork before each chair, but the fact that the chairman, Lord Blenshaw, would be attending the meeting in just over one hour's time. Meanwhile it was suggested they sit down, and study the contract that now lay before them, for it was to the problems concerning this contract, that this meeting was called, and from which they needed some answers.

It was almost lunchtime before Lord Blenshaw returned, by then Jamie had gone over the contract several times, puzzled as to why this vast complex was given to them to study, when it was clearly marked as part of an American project, the whole operation taking place between four states in central America, linking them together by road, rail and a series of bridges and tunnels, plus turning a nondescript harbour into a major port, complete with oil terminal.

Lord Blenshaw's opening words put what Jamie had suspected about this package in a nutshell, whether it was mistrust of their northern neighbours giving them a hard sell, or inexperience. The American side of their company had mishandled the signing of this billion dollar contract, leaving the four participants very wary of the situation. The whole project was now in danger of collapsing, although he could see, and he had no doubt, that the people concerned could also see the benefits this vast contract would bring to the region as a whole, they were now looking for ways to resolve this situation by taking on the signing if possible. Certainly they would like to recover the finance they'd already spent, but most importantly, as Lord Blenshaw stated, to see that the good name of the company remained intact.

As the discussion moved on, Jamie soon became aware that being the most experienced person around the table the onus was on him so, without too much of a delay, he informed the chair of his retirement date.

"Thank you for pointing that out, Sir," Lord Blenshaw said, "and you are right to assume that we have you in mind to take this assignment onboard, although of course you are free to refuse, but at the same time we would appreciate your thoughts on this request for assistance, and to what you'd require in an operation such as this."

Jamie hesitated, and then spelt out his thoughts. "This project has an element of corruption within it. I'm sure they like what's being offered to them, but the leader of each of the interested parties seemed to have a wish to declare themselves anything other than a shared member, so I feel a great deal of caution is needed, and with that this is what I would require on such a venture. Firstly I need someone to accompany me – I suggest Peter Bradley – secondly there has to be extra insurance, thirdly I would require a company jet at my disposal, not just to get us there, but to get us out fast if it was found necessary, and lastly I would require a bank of ten million dollars, to put a smile where there are none at present."

With a nod of agreement at each request Lord Blenshaw asked him if there was anything else he needed.

"Just the approval of my wife," he said.

"In that case you'd better bring her along to dinner," Lord Blenshaw replied.

In fact, Jamie had his dinner at home that night with Amy; if there was anything to discuss about this assignment he preferred to go through it with her. After a bit of soul-searching, and his assurance of not remaining out there longer than necessary, and most certainly not after his retirement date, she gave him her blessing.

Winging his way across the Atlantic in a business jet with a four-man crew, Jamie was furious with himself for being talked into this job, and at people like Lord Blenshaw – if he thought he was joking about seeking Amy's approval he was bloody well wrong; if she'd have wavered a little, he'd have told them to stuff it. He'd spent too many years reaching for her hand in some shabby hotel, and finding only a briefcase full of problems, and now at the wrong end of his life he was being plunged into an unholy mess amongst excitable volatile people who only really wanted the same peaceful life as he did, but had been pushed harder than necessary, leading them into a vacuum of uncertainty. He knew their only hope now was to smile a lot and act politely, even though they would be jostled and try and take the steam out of the situation before talking business.

They were booked into a Hilton Hotel within easy reach of the airport. He was more than happy with that, plus the hotel contained a large conference room in which most of the general meetings would take place – a promising start, he thought.

After an introductory general meeting, in which the climate made it hot and sticky, he decided to hold smaller meetings touring all four states travelling by air. It proved hard going, and they were glad to make it back to the hotel each night, but by the end of four days, he knew he had the right man in Peter Bradley who mixed well, and his Spanish was excellent.

By their softly softly approach Jamie had a feeling he was gaining ground. He sat and listened to them, answering their questions, discussing their problems, problems that were not entirely to do with the contract, and by the end of the fourth day he knew that they themselves would come to a decision and sign.

The phone by the side of his bed awoke him – it was dark, and a quick glance at his watch told him it was 4 a.m. Picking it up he caught his breath at the sound of Verlisity's voice; it was something like 9 a.m. over there. "I expect I woke you, Father, but I had to catch you," she said.

"A problem?" he enquired.

"Please do not get into a panic and make yourself ill, but Mother's been involved in an accident – just a few small cuts and bruises, but of course badly shaken. I have her in a nursing home quite near to our house."

"What happened?" he said.

"She went back to Cumbria to check on the background music for that film, and on the way home the coach left the road and turned over. She was wearing a seatbelt which saved her," she replied.

"My God," he said, "don't let her know, but I'll be over. I'll leave here within the hour, and will call you from the plane to pick me up."

"Thank you, Father, I love you," and she rang off, leaving him staring down at the phone as though it was some evil spirit. He just hoped the pilot hadn't been on a binge, because he needed him now.

He awoke Peter and explained the situation to him, asking him to hold the fort for at least twenty-four hours, making any excuse he deemed plausible as to his absence. He roused the pilot and, with the plane already on standby as agreed, he was away at 5 a.m.

Once airborne with Pilot, Co-Pilot, Flight Engineer, and Steward who fixed him up with coffee and a bite to eat, he put them in the picture, plus the quick turnaround they would have to make, which was something he was given to understand was not unusual in the company business and he gave a silent prayer for that.

A slightly subdued yet typical Verlisity greeted him at the airport with a hug and a kiss. Once at the nursing home she led him towards her mother's room, opened the door, and ushered him in but remained outside. Amy was sitting in a chair facing the window, and as he approached she turned and started to rise at the sight of him. He stopped her and fell onto his knees before her, hugging her to him, showering her with his kisses.

"Oh, Jamie, my love," she cried out, "I'm so sorry, I shouldn't have gone out there, there was no need."

"Hush, my love," he countered, "you wouldn't have been happy if you didn't, I know that," he said. "We're two of a kind, you and I, things have to be right or not at all, but it's over now, my love, you've crossed the last hurdle and your safe thank God."

"But you haven't, darling, have you? You have to go back," she said.

"I'm afraid so, my dear," he added. "But not for long I'm sure. You and I have a date to keep – remember?' she nodded at that. "You know," he continued, letting his eyes direct her gaze towards the door where Verlisity stood, "we'll never be completely on our own, dear." She smiled at that, looking more like his real Amy at that point.

"I know," she whispered. "The pretty little key that opened the door for us will always be there, both in our minds, and in our hearts."

Sitting back in the seat on the plane, he felt a lot happier with himself having seen Amy, and the fact that he was on his way back to fulfil his last commitment with the company. Looking around at the small number of seats, tables, and computers it was a flying office, built for companies such as Glo-Tec; he'd travelled on them before, but never had he been more thankful than he was at that moment in its use, and not in the least bit guilty of doing so.

He had to force his mind back from the thoughts of Amy to the task that lay ahead. He knew he was gaining their confidence in him, they were beginning to smile more often, and laugh when he laughed, but at the general meetings there was always the unnecessary air of suspicion towards each other, and to find an answer to that is what he required right now.

It was like a hand placed on his shoulder as his thoughts led him to Sir Jacob, standing there in his study, explaining to him the various tactics used in business transactions. "It's all about division and multiplication, dear boy, divide and multiply," as he said it over and over again, he almost burst out laughing. "You were a wise old bird," he muttered, "that's the key I need."

He'd left in the dark, and now twenty-four hours later he was back in it, and despite all the joy he'd felt at seeing Amy again, there was still anger; on stepping down from this flying office into the hot, steamy, bug-laden atmosphere once more, it was threatening to well up inside of him. He felt as though he should have phoned up the office and told them to stuff the bloody job. Was this contract really worth saving, he asked himself, his mind being torn apart with angry words from the people he was dealing with, taking the stick for someone else's cock-up. He knew it was a good contract, it was right for the people as a whole, there was work for them there, work to enjoy life, get married, and raise a family. What would Alex his father think of it all? Would he walk away? No he bloody well wouldn't, he'd sort it. Today he'd start the ball rolling, if the plan he had in mind based on his thoughts of Sir Jacob failed, then that would really be the end of the line.

He shaved, showered, put on a change of clothing, and made himself a mug of coffee from the tray in the room. Sitting down at the desk they had provided, he set down the number of questions he needed to ask, then at first light he awoke Peter, giving him as much gen as possible before calling up the company's legal team.

The anger that was in him stripped away the years, it was JP out there now in full flow, he wasn't asking them anything, he was telling them. They all had to be in the conference room at 11 a.m. sharp, complete with the plans of the new port, right down to the last detail. He needed to get a clear picture of the railway, its station and marshalling yard, the new road system and its terminal within the dock area, plus the docks with all their facilities and, most important of all, the concerning party to which he called plan A, with the authority to sign up for this contract, to sit down with him at a working lunch, and listen to what he had to say, and it was to them only he needed to address and them only.

Coffee was served as they took their seats around the table. He informed them that he didn't want any questions put to him at that moment, and with the aid of a large screen onto which the plans were clearly visible, he began speaking. Raising or lowering the tone of his voice as he found necessary, moving over the plans like some skilled surgeon, dissecting them in the same explanatory way that had drawn Sir Richard's attention to him nearly forty years ago, making slight suggestions where he deemed possible without any additional cost, it was when he spoke of the general improvements covering four states, and backed by the world bank, he caught several nods of acceptance, and decided it was a good time to go for lunch.

The lunch took less than one hour with the conversation flowing well on all sides, and once back to the conference room he endured a further half an hour of questions before standing up to make his final speech, and playing what Sir Jacob would call his final trump card.

"Gentlemen," he said, "thank you for hearing me out, and your interest in putting those questions to me, of which I hope I gave you some satisfactory answers, but now I must apologize for the lack of information you were given in the first instance. This is not the way this great company runs its business, adding to that I have the authority to hand you a cheque of two million dollars as a gesture of good will, and faith in Glo-Tec-Associates." Handing over the cheque he added, "If you wish to confer with us further this afternoon, we will be in the mezzanine."

It was at 4 p.m. when they were called back into the conference room. There were still a few more questions and points of view to be ironed out before their chairman stood up and reached for Jamie's hand, and the contract was duly signed.

It had been a hard day for them all, but as Jamie reminded them, they had to keep up the momentum or else the whole idea would collapse around them. As it was, it took a further four days of working lunches, and a multitude of questions to be answered, where problem after problem was presented to them. Plus in each case the gift of two million dollars, until the last and final contract was signed.

Being late in the day, and completely drained, Jamie and Peter made it back to the hotel, filled in their report as required, and made the decision to rest and fly home tomorrow.

It was late in the afternoon when the company car drew up outside of The Park. For Jamie the journey back from Central America seemed to have taken forever, but at last he was beginning to feel he'd finally made it. Turning in his seat he grasped the hand of Peter Bradley, and shook it firmly.

"Well this is as far as I go, young man," he said. "Thank you for your most valued assistance out there, I hope you found the experience interesting," he chuckled.

"Thank you, Sir, for inviting me," Peter said. "I enjoyed it, bugs and all."

At that point Jamie handed his briefcase to him saying, "It's all yours from now on, Peter, my compliments to Lord Blenshaw and the office, and as from this moment I'm retired."

Entering the flat he tossed his holdall into the cloak cupboard to be sorted later. Removing his jacket, he turned to see the smiling face of Verlisity standing there. She put her arms around him saying, "Welcome home, Father, I've some tea ready, go and sit down, I'll be with you in a moment or two."

"Mother," he questioned, "is she home?"

"No, Father, but she's fine, I'll explain it all to you over tea."

He was still standing vaguely gazing around when Verlisity arrived with the tea tray, to set it down upon the small table, her brief words of comfort to him as regards to Amy was perhaps not quite enough, not for the almost childlike excitement that was flowing through his body, this feeling of escapism, which they'd both dreamed of, still seemed so far away without her smiling face before him now and he was struggling to overcome his emotions.

Verlisity's request for him to sit down brought him back into reality with a jolt. He obeyed, and watched her pour out the tea; sitting down beside him she said, "Are you alright, Father? You look a little tired."

"Just a bit," he replied. "Now what's this with Mother that you have to explain, my dear, she's surely not working?"

"Most definitely not," she replied. "Now just hear me out."

Slipping her arm under his, taking his hand, and squeezing it, Verlisity began to put into words her thoughts of the past, present, and the future. She spoke of the holidays they'd had together, but also the many times when there had been just one of them there. She'd never stopped loving them for that, she understood how their life was run, she said her mother told her how he'd turn up at the stage door in various parts of the world just to let her know he cared, and how she would do the same, he chuckled over that. "But now, Father," she said, "this is the present and our future. I want you, Mother, Johnathan, and the children to become a real family, there will be no missing members anymore, and we will stand as one, and do most things together."

After a brief pause she said, "And now to Mother, and where she is at this moment. You know, Father, there has to be a special reason for her to be there, she spoke of a beginning to which you would understand, I would also at some point like to understand, Father..." It was then she placed a small photograph in front of him of a stone-built, thatched roof crofter's cabin. "Mother's there, it's in the Western Isles, Father."

"Tess," he said looking down at it, "The Isle of Tess." She nodded, bending forward cupping his face in his hands to hide the tears welling there, he murmured, "Amy, Amy, my love, of course I understand, how could I not." Sitting up again to put his arm around Verlisity he said, "This is a past that will always be the present, and the future, and the word is love. You were there, darling, Mother was four months pregnant with you, we ran away from those who wanted our very souls, spending four glorious days and nights there,

114

amongst such lovely people, sharing their land, sea, sky, and the wind, the wind that freshens the air to make it as pure as an angel's breath, sandy golden enclaves, with grassy brows where we could sit or lay in peace, to share our love, and in the evenings we'd fill our dreams to the lilting sounds of some Gaelic love songs. We almost never came back, but we needed you to have a good life, to get the best out of it, to find a good man, and have a family. You've achieved all that, and given us a deeper meaning to love itself. Now go home to that young man of yours, and give the little ones a hug from Grandpa, whilst I make plans for tomorrow, and will call you on our return."

Although so many years had passed by, the magic of those four stolen days had never left Amy, or himself for that matter. It was a dream that lived and would go on living, and he was not about to destroy it by rushing headlong down to the cabin, and carrying her off to the nearest boat, and with all the joy they'd found in this Isle – that would not be Amy's wish, nor his either. So with the information he'd been given by Verlisity as to what she had taken with her, plus a number to contact a certain Mrs Mary MacDonald, whose son Alister was running errands for Amy, and who on phoning had kindly agreed to him using her little abode as their meeting place, with a further request from him to provide a meal for them that evening, he could then make his plans to bring her home, or stay a while longer if she so wished. It would be her decision, and hers alone, as it was in the past when she finally accepted his proposal of marriage. It was to be a new beginning she had said, and now there was to be another – the last.

When he awoke that morning from an uncertain sleep upon the settee, still fully dressed, a sleep in which his mind had raced through every twist and turn of their lives, he fully understood why she had gone back to Tess; their dreams were still there, and when they finally returned, they would come with them, no one would ever take them away again, they would be theirs forever.

A small private plane took him north to a nearby Isle, and from there a motorboat ferried him across the sound and alongside the stone and timber jetty of Tess itself where at the shoreline Mrs Mary MacDonald, a smiling carbon copy of Mrs Double D, was waiting for him. Sensing the significance of the occasion, she was full of excitable chatter as she led him through a collection of mainly single-storey dwellings to her own, where he was ushered through a heavy door made from old ships' timbers into a room that embraced him with its charm, and a sense of homeliness, a room that was many rooms in one, with the kitchen range set well back into a deep recess and upon which their evening meal was in the process of being cooked.

She showed him around her home, including the main bedroom which she had prepared for them if they wished to sleep there, as she with her son would be sleeping elsewhere that night. This was something Jamie in his eagerness to see Amy hadn't contemplated, but he thanked her for it.

Whilst in the kitchen area to check on the meal, and to assure him that it would be ready in time for him to serve, a red-haired young lad entered the room. Calling him over, Mary introduced him to Jamie, "This is my son Alister," she said.

Jamie shook his hand, and said, "Hello, Alister, the very young man I wanted to see." Opening the long box he'd brought with him, he lifted out from it a spray of yellow carnations, checking the card on it which read, *My dearest Amy, love of my life, I'm here darling, dinner at 7 p.m. J.* Handing it to Alister he said, "Please would you kindly take these to my wife, and then return to give me any message, or perhaps just a smile," and that was exactly what he saw in Alister when he returned, and he knew she would be there.

Just as her footsteps stopped he opened the door, they stood looking at each other for a brief moment in complete silence. She was wearing a pale pink chiffon dress with three-quarter sleeves, the neckline and cuffs edged into a series of fluffy loose folds. His heart skipped a beat, this was for all the world his Amy, his princess.

She took his hand as he guided her over the threshold, and across the room into the light of the window, where they stopped and turned to face each other. At that point there was no need for words, for when they finally came, they would be straight from the heart. They were there to appraise their dreams, and gain strength from them for the way ahead. They knew they belonged, they had confirmed that in so may ways, they had nothing to prove to anyone but themselves, and only themselves.

He looked at her unlined beautiful face, framed within those dancing locks, now as snowy-white as his own, those soft brown eyes, a little quieter now, and those lips that concealed a smile as bright as the brightest star, lips that had led him into pastures new where his doubts could be calmed, and his purpose in life fulfilled, now awaiting his own.

She was also wearing his gift of the gold necklace and earrings which she knew he enjoyed seeing her wear. He wasn't sure how he missed it when she came through the door, or even when they first turned to face each other, but suddenly it was there in all its glory, flashing like a brilliant green beacon. He moved his eyes towards it, and gasped – high on her left shoulder was the brooch, the bond of love. He hadn't seen it in all these years, as he looked into it he saw the face of a young girl with glossy chestnut hair, with a smile that was filling the room with light, and dancing with his heart. His eyes were misting over and something seemed to be marking his face. He raised his hand to brush it away, she took it, and pulled him towards her. He saw the tears welling in her eyes, putting his hand around her waist he drew her to him, placing his lips upon the tears feeling the saltiness, then onto her cheeks, and finally onto her lips as she herself drew him tighter to her.

The great tide of time rushed over them, crashing upon their shore in all its fury of a thousand and one days and nights, searching out the pain of youth's desire denied, the pain of longing, the pain of watching, yet daring to seek an answer. The pain, oh so many pains of those constant partings, on and on they fled from them, sweeping the flotsam that crowded their paths, and casting it deep into the ocean's bed forever, until slowly ever so slowly receding, to be but a ripple upon the water's edge, leaving a clear untouched expanse of golden sand that sparkled in the sunlight, clean, and crisp as the page of a new book.

Lifting his head from her shoulder, with a voice full of the emotions within his body, he said, "It's time, Amy my love, let's go home."

Her whispered voice came sweet to his ear. "Oh, Jamie. Yes, my darling, yes."

Not quite the end...

Epilogue

Just a mile or two north of Fern Bridge where the river narrows, on its western flank lies an area of open parkland, with a children's play centre, whilst on the opposite side there are botanical gardens, a pretty footbridge crosses the river at that point, its metallic sides were designed into a series of green leaves, and yellow-headed flowers. The inscription on the plaque at either end of the bridge reads, *Amy's Bridge*.

The end of the story, but never of love.